Holden

INK AND EMBER

BOOK ONE

KATE HAWTHORNE

Holden: Ink and Ember #1
by Kate Hawthorne

Copyright © 2026
Kate Hawthorne

Edited by | Jordan Buchanan
Cover Design | Amai Designs

HOLDEN AND BRYCE

Holden

INK AND EMBER BOOK ONE

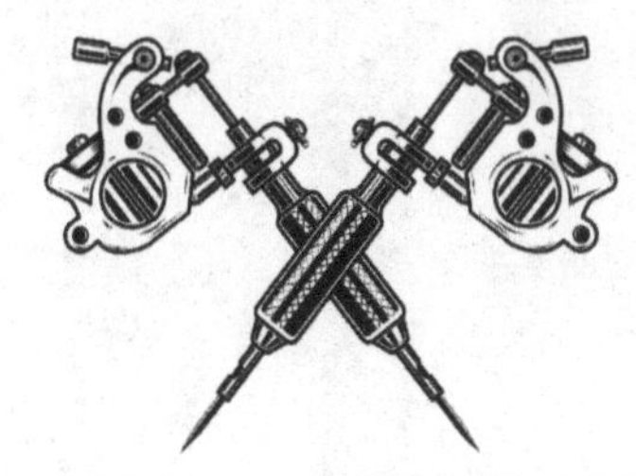

KATE HAWTHORNE

CHAPTER 1

Holden

HOLDEN WALKER ENJOYED ALMOST everything about his life. He had a studio apartment in Hollywood he'd been locked into for almost ten years, he knew how to cook more than spaghetti and stir fry, and most importantly of all, he was single. He also scored the gig of a lifetime working at Ink and Ember, a small tattoo shop on the outskirts of a residential neighborhood in Silverlake.

All in all, it was a good life, if not a sometimes lonely one. But if he ever found himself wanting for conversation or company, the only thing he had to do was go into the shop. The tattooer who worked in the booth right beside him, Merrick Shannon, hadn't stopped talking since the day he was born and had no problem carrying a conversation for the both of them.

At first, it had made Holden feel like he was losing his mind. The constant chatter had him on edge, and he'd come home many days in the first months of his employment wondering if he'd made a mistake. He'd gone to bed knowing he hadn't, that working for Riggs Ember was a great gig, and as far as coworkers went, he could have done worse. Merrick might have talked a lot, but he was polite and he kept his space clean, *and* he was a great tattooer.

That was what Holden kept reminding himself as he cleaned and bandaged his second-to-last client for the day, the incessant rattle of Merrick's voice an ever-present hum in the back of his mind.

"Leave it on overnight if you can. At least until bedtime," Holden told his client, tearing off the last bit of tape and pressing it onto her skin. "Then it's unscented antibacterial soap and nothing else. Simple white lotion after two days whenever it gets dry or tight or itchy."

The buzz of Merrick's tattoo machine died down and his voice filtered over to Holden's booth.

"I don't get why you haven't switched to Saniderm," Merrick said.

Holden clenched his jaw. "It's not how I was taught."

"Not how I was taught either."

"Plastic wrap has worked fine for years." He held his tattooed arm out as proof. "I think it will keep working for a few more."

"I'm allergic to it anyway," Holden's client, Ashley, piped up. "So this is good."

Holden scratched the tip of his nose, hoping his hand obscured enough of his face to hide his smile. He wasn't trying to be smug about being right, but he did appreciate having his methods validated. He finished up with Ashley, thanked her for the generous tip, then returned to his station to get cleaned up.

Merrick had started chittering away again, such an unrelenting flow of words Holden didn't hear the bells on the door jingle to alert them a new customer arrived. It wasn't until said customer knocked on the counter with tattooed knuckles that Holden looked up. Merrick cut his machine at the same time, a frustratingly bright smile splitting his face when he saw the customer.

"Bryce." Merrick snapped off his gloves and glanced at his client. "I'll be right back. My brother just got here."

When Merrick made it around the counter, the family resemblance was impossible to miss. Merrick and Bryce were practically the same height, just on the right side of six foot, same build, slender without being scrawny, strong without being overtly muscular. They both had the same shade of dark hair, though Bryce's was styled in a taper cut, compared to Merrick's floppy brown waves that looked like they would have been more in place in the late nineties than any other time. The only real difference was Bryce looked how Holden would have imagined Merrick did ten years earlier. Obviously the younger brother between the two of them, his appearance something Holden found himself all too focused on.

Holden bit his lips together between his teeth and narrowed his eyes, wondering what was wrong with him. He'd never looked at Merrick with any sort of interest at all, but his brother…that was another story entirely.

He turned his attention to wiping down his chair, ear turned toward the counter in a way that would let him eavesdrop without looking like it. His older sister would be proud of him.

"When did you get into town?" Merrick asked.

"Just now," Bryce answered.

"I told you I'd pick you up from the airport."

"I wanted to surprise you. Caught an earlier flight."

"Well, I'm surprised," Merrick said, glancing over his shoulder at his client, the massive thigh tattoo still hours away from being finished. "But I'm also stuck here for the foreseeable future."

"You're fine," Bryce assured Merrick. "I just wanted to come by and say hello. I can take a car back to your place and we can get together for dinner just like we planned."

"I don't want you to have to pay for another ride."

"I really don't mind," Bryce said. "But I am starving. Is there anywhere around here I can grab a bite to eat? Can I maybe leave my bag?"

"Yes to both," Merrick answered, his stare finally shifting far enough across the room to land on me. "Holden."

Holden looked at him, brow raised.

"When's your next client?" he asked.

"Not for an hour."

"Can you walk my brother down to the deli on the corner?" Merrick reached into his pocket and pulled out forty bucks, shoving it at Bryce before he could protest. "Make sure he eats."

"I'm twenty-two," Bryce argued, tossing the money on the counter. "I don't need a babysitter, I just need directions." His stare flickered to Holden, eyes darkening.

"Need to finish cleaning," Holden said, and Merrick scoffed at him.

"You're clean. I gave him enough for both of you. Please? I know he can do it alone." Merrick looked at his brother. "I know you can do it alone, but it's your first time in LA—"

"If I can make it out of LAX, which I did, I think I can manage a walk down to a deli on the corner."

"Not this corner," Holden interrupted, clenching his jaw and immediately regretting getting involved.

Two matching brown stares drifted toward him, and he took a deep breath. "It's..."

He gave up explaining and gestured weakly toward the neighborhood behind the shop.

"I can take directions," Bryce said.

Holden had to turn away at that point, not wanting either man to see his face.

"Please, Holden?" Merrick asked.

"Sure." He tossed the paper towel he'd been cleaning with into the trash and put some sanitizer on his hands.

"I don't need an escort," Bryce said again.

"What if he's hungry too?" Merrick countered, knocking into Holden with his elbow as he headed toward the counter. "Are you hungry, Holden?"

"Holden," Bryce murmured the name, and when Holden looked at the other man, Bryce pursed his lips like he hadn't meant to be heard.

"I could eat," he finally said.

Merrick grinned, and Holden couldn't get a read on Bryce's expression. For as similar as they were, he was quickly spotting the differences between them.

"Holden isn't big on conversation," Merrick said over his shoulder. "Don't take it personally."

"We can't all be as chatty as you are, brother."

Holden snatched the forty dollars off the counter and stuffed it into his pocket.

"Let me get your bag," Merrick said.

Bryce passed his bag to his brother, they talked some more, and it gave Holden more than enough time to second-guess whether agreeing to walk Bryce to the deli was a good idea or not. Tired of waiting, he pushed open the door to the shop and stepped outside. The mid-afternoon air was warm, and he leaned against the brick wall of the building to wait for Bryce to finish talking with Merrick—which likely would never happen.

Five minutes later, Bryce did appear, though, a curious smile on his face and a subtle tilt to his head that Holden thought looked like trouble.

"Ready?" Holden asked.

"Wherever you lead, I'll follow."

A swell of heat rolled through Holden, and he ignored the comment entirely, pushing off the wall and heading down the block. Behind him, Bryce chuckled and jogged to catch up. Once they fell into step together, Bryce immediately started talking and Holden wondered if it would literally kill the Shannon brothers to ever be quiet.

"Do you ever stop talking?" he asked, turning the corner, grateful the deli was finally in sight.

"If someone puts something in my mouth, sure."

He shot Bryce a sidelong glance.

"I can show you, if you want," Bryce added.

Holden's tongue stuck to the roof of his mouth, throat suddenly as dry as the Sahara desert. He didn't have a single decent thing to say, so he said nothing at all. But, damn, how long had it been since he'd fucked? How long since he'd even messed around with someone? Months, probably. He wasn't in the habit of counting or keeping track, but he knew it had been a pretty thorough dry spell. And not for lack of interest, maybe just a lack of motivation. After a long day at work, he appreciated the quiet of his apartment. The last thing Holden wanted to do was go out and make more superficial conversation with someone, all under the guise of getting off at the end of the night.

"Excuse me?"

They came to a stop in front of the deli on the corner. The sliding window that faced the street was slid open, the small handwritten menu taped onto the glass.

"I don't talk with my mouth full," Bryce said, eyes twinkling as he leaned in to presumably read the menu. "And we're about to get lunch, so…"

"Hardly lunchtime," Holden said.

"Definitely not dinner."

"A weird in-between thing, then."

Bryce straightened up and grinned at him like whatever Holden had just said was the sweetest or funniest thing he had ever heard in his life. Holden ignored the way the look made him feel and shoved his hands into his pockets.

"What do you like, Holden?" Bryce asked, pausing before tilting his head toward the building. "To eat, I mean."

Words were never his strong suit, but being around Bryce made them ten times harder to make sense of. "The Italian."

"We're Greek," Bryce said. "And Irish. If you wanted to know."

The younger man turned toward the window and leaned down to order. "Two Italians please." He glanced over his shoulder. "Drink?"

Holden opened his mouth to speak but words again failed him. Not because he didn't want to have the conversation but because Bryce was giving him whiplash. Holden couldn't decide whether he liked the man or hated him, but his body was giving very clear signals about where he stood physically on the matter. Back at the shop, Holden had certainly had some impure thoughts about getting Bryce onto his knees, but there was something so appealing about the casual way Bryce steered a conversation in his favor that had Holden feeling some other sort of way entirely.

He cleared his throat and answered, "Coke is fine."

"Two Cokes," Bryce ordered, reaching behind him and making a gimme motion with his hand.

Holden pulled the money out of his pocket and pressed it into Bryce's waiting palm, doing his best to ignore the burning heat of Bryce's skin and the way it set Holden's entire body aflame.

CHAPTER 2

Bryce

"SO, YOU'RE A TALKER," Bryce said, seconds before cramming the biggest Italian sub he'd ever seen into his mouth. Holden had already chewed and swallowed his first bite, and instead of answering with words, he flicked his gaze up at Bryce in a way that would have certainly taken his legs out from under him if he'd been standing.

His brother wasn't wrong about Holden. The man was insanely attractive, with bleached hair that had started to grow out and reveal dark roots, round cheeks and a plush mouth, a slim body that was definitely covered in more tattoos than Bryce could currently see. Merrick had told him all about the shop, about Riggs—the guy who owned it—and about Holden, the grumpy and brooding artist who worked beside him. He'd told Bryce about the beach and the weather and the tacos, and from the first day Merrick had gotten hired, getting Bryce to California had been the plan.

"Sarcasm noted," Holden murmured, tucking in for another bite of his late lunch. Bryce followed suit, trying to not stare too long at the shape of Holden's jaw as he chewed or the flex of his throat when he swallowed.

"This is good." He wiped his mouth with the back of his

hand and set the sub down on the white paper wrapper he'd unfolded to use as a plate. Some lettuce and red onions had already fallen out of the overstuffed sandwich, and he popped one of the onion slivers into his mouth to make sure he didn't do something careless like get ideas about kissing strangers.

The thing was, though…Bryce liked kissing strangers. He liked kissing everybody.

"Are you from here?" he asked.

Holden glanced up at him and set down his sandwich, wiping his hands on a napkin before dropping them into his lap. "Yes."

"Do you like it?"

"Obviously."

"How long have you been tattooing for?"

"Since I was nineteen," Holden answered.

"How many years is that?"

Holden licked his lips, pink tongue darting out and drawing a slick line Bryce couldn't help but stare at. How was he supposed to stay strong in the face of such a gorgeous man? What had Merrick been thinking sending them out to eat? He knew how Bryce could be sometimes, and Bryce was a little tired from the flight, from the stress of the trip, from his entire life.

"Do you and your brother ever stop talking?"

Bryce's mouth twitched and he scratched his Cupid's bow with the corner of a jagged fingernail. "My answer is the same as before."

Holden studied him, and Bryce had to look away. The weight of Holden's crystalline blue stare was too much for him to handle on as little sleep as he'd gotten the night before. The man was objectively gorgeous, and Bryce didn't have much willpower when it came to telling pretty men no.

"My brother talks more than me," Bryce explained. "He started early and never stopped, and if I ever wanted to be heard at home I had to have just as many words and just as much volume."

"Doesn't it ever get tiring?"

Holden hadn't looked away from him, a few loose strands of hair falling into his eyes. Bryce picked up his sandwich and took another bite, chewing and swallowing before answering, "Yes."

Competing with Merrick had always been exhausting, but it was the only way to be seen in their house, growing up. Merrick had not only excelled in academics but also art. He was social and he was friendly; everybody loved him. Bryce hadn't necessarily grown up in Merrick's shadow, but there were absolutely some big—albeit hand-me-down—shoes to fill.

"Then why don't you stop?" Holden asked.

Bryce let out a low laugh, scrubbing a hand down his face. "At this point, I don't think I know how."

"I could think of a couple ways," Holden said.

Bryce's eyes went wide, a surge of something flaring out from his stomach and tickling every nerve in his body. The reaction must have been visible because Holden smirked before covering the lower half of his face with his hand and looking away.

The conversation felt like an impasse...or maybe an invitation. Bryce wasn't entirely sure, but the thing about growing up with a brother like Merrick meant he always had to at least try.

"Tell me more?" he asked.

Bryce would have sworn Holden's cheeks darkened, but it could have also been a shadow. There were so many palm trees in Los Angeles. It was one of the first things he'd noticed on the ride from the airport. Well, that and all the concrete. Los Angeles wasn't anything like the small town in Colorado he'd grown up in, and maybe that was part of the appeal.

Merrick leaving had been a blessing and a curse. For as

much as Bryce had struggled to get a footing in his own life, he found it ten times harder to do the same with his brother gone. He could have dropped out of college and moved early, or transferred his credits or something, but with all the chatting and all the brain power, Merrick had always also been Bryce's voice of reason.

Don't walk away from the scholarship, his brother had told him.

So he hadn't.

Add the minor if you can handle the course load, his brother had said.

So he did.

"No," Holden said softly, wrapping the remainder of his sandwich back into the wrapper and carefully pressing the tape back down to seal it closed.

Bryce cursed under his breath.

"Sorry."

"For what?"

"Saying that," Bryce answered. "Obviously, it wasn't welcome."

"Not unwelcome," Holden said, standing from the rusted iron table and angling his head toward the direction of Ink and Ember. "Just short on time."

Bryce made less graceful work of wrapping up his sandwich and untangling himself from the table. Holden had already started to walk back to work, and Bryce jogged to catch up to him. They fell in step together, and that was maybe the first time he realized Holden was shorter than him. Not by much, but enough that if they ever did kiss, he would have to tilt his head down...

"Short on time," he repeated. "Does that mean...?"

"It means I have another appointment I have to set up for."

"And after?"

Holden took a breath that lifted his shoulders, and Bryce

watched him hold it. He counted to five until Holden exhaled, and they both turned a corner, the shop once again in sight. He didn't think this was the last time he would see Holden, but he was running out of time in this specific moment and he wasn't quite ready to let it slip away.

"Are you staying with your brother?" Holden asked.

"That was the plan."

"Then nothing," he said.

"Why nothing?"

"Because you have no reason to go out on your own just yet, and I have no reason to come over to his place. I don't even know where he lives."

"How do you…" Bryce stopped himself from finishing the thought. "Actually, never mind."

Holden shot him an unimpressed look.

"Merrick is a lot," Bryce said, and Holden scoffed. "It would be very reasonable for me to tell him I need a breather."

"Not your first day here."

"You clearly don't know Merrick," he shot back.

The shop was closer, close enough Bryce could read the dark black and bronze logo on the window. He took a risk and grabbed Holden's wrist, dragging the other man to a stop. They both stared down at the way Bryce's tattooed fingers curled around Holden's tattooed wrist, and neither of them said a word for so long Bryce almost forgot to breathe.

"I think I like you more when you're quiet," Holden said, taking his hand back.

"I can be quiet," Bryce said. "I actually…sometimes I prefer it."

Holden swallowed, visibly and audibly, and Bryce fought the urge to lean down and see if he could taste the vinaigrette on Holden's mouth.

"What's on your knuckles?" Holden asked, which might have been the absolute last thing Bryce expected him to ask.

He frowned, looking down at his own hands like he'd forgotten the tattoos there. He made fists of his hands and showed the ink to Holden, who nodded approvingly.

"Stardust," he said, tracing his finger in a straight line across the bold letters. "Why?"

"We're made of it."

Holden licked his lips, wetting them in a borderline indecent way before pulling them both into his mouth and biting down. God, did the man have any idea how attractive he was? He had to know, right? There was no way Holden didn't realize the effect he had on people, or at the very least the effect he was having on Bryce.

"I wanted a reminder that I'm more than this," he added softly. "And also less."

Holden released his lips, teeth marks visible.

"Give me your phone," Holden said, extending his hand.

Bryce knew a chance when he saw it, and he had his phone out of his pocket embarrassingly quickly. He dropped the device in Holden's waiting palm, mouth twitching into a smile when Holden held it up facing him so the screen would unlock. The other man scrolled through the apps Bryce had open, which hadn't been anything interesting. His photo gallery from the airplane ride after the Wi-Fi had cut out, a game he'd been playing while he'd waited to board, a book he'd been reading, a streaming app with a documentary he'd grown bored of. Holden flicked his stare up to Bryce and hesitated before continuing his search.

"I don't have anything indecent, if that's what you're looking for," he said. "I mean, there is an album, but it's hidden."

Holden chuckled and swiped through to Bryce's text messages. He started a new thread and keyed in a phone number Bryce very much hoped was his, sent a message, then held the phone out for him to take. Bryce didn't even look at it. He returned his phone to his pocket and tried to not smile at Holden like he'd just won the lottery.

"Would it be too forward if I told you I haven't been able to stop thinking about how much I want to kiss you since the first moment you opened your mouth?" Bryce asked.

"Maybe."

"Well, I have."

Holden licked his lips and did that thing again where he bit down on the bottom one. Bryce reached up, ready to draw it out of his mouth but moved too slow. It was already free by the time his hand got there, but he pressed his thumb against Holden's lip anyway, pulling it down just enough to expose his teeth. Holden didn't stop him, but the things Bryce wanted to do next—or have done to him, more fittingly—were not appropriate for the sidewalk, so he pulled his hand back and crossed his arms in front of his chest.

"I'm gonna text you later tonight," he said.

Holden studied him, but it was like the proximity to the shop had drawn the man back into his shell. Instead of words, he nodded and turned away, walking the last half of the block alone. Bryce waited until Holden had disappeared into the shop to check his cell phone. He smiled to himself when he found Holden's contact information saved, and a text message thread open and ready for him to start.

CHAPTER 3

Holden

HOLDEN MANAGED to get through the rest of his shift, letting the buzz of his tattoo machine drown out the sound of Merrick's never-ending chatter. When he'd gotten back from lunch, Bryce had taken his bag and a spare key from Merrick and left. But that didn't mean Holden was able to stop thinking about him. In fact, quite the opposite. He'd been so distracted by thoughts of Merrick's younger brother that he barely noticed when Riggs, his boss and the owner of the shop, showed up, boyfriend in tow. Riggs and Smith said hello to everyone before going upstairs, and Holden and Merrick both glanced at the ceiling as soon as the door closed.

Riggs was a good boss and an even better tattooer. It was Riggs's best friend who had approached him first about taking a booth at the shop. Damon said Riggs was a stubborn son of a bitch who was ready to bring in some staff but wasn't ready to do the work to get there. Damon had apparently scoured the city to collect portfolios which he then dropped in front of his best friend until Riggs made the decision for himself on expanding the shop.

Holden and Merrick were the two lucky artists, but there was an empty spot tucked into the back corner of the shop still waiting to be filled. Because of their location, the shop didn't get a ton of walk-in clientele, but it wasn't unheard of. Smith had been a walk-in, and that had turned into much more than a repeat client. Stranger things had and would continue to happen.

Like Bryce, he told himself.

He had no business flirting with Merrick's little brother. It was one thing to go out and fuck a stranger, another to fuck the sibling of your coworker. Holden didn't even particularly *like* Merrick. He didn't dislike the man, but the talking really was over the top sometimes, and Bryce, while also unable to quiet down for more than a minute at a time, resonated a little differently with Holden. It was possible, Holden thought, that he could maybe quiet Bryce down long enough to kiss him. If Bryce texted him, which would probably be a bad idea. Because of Merrick.

But did that really matter?

He thought about the pros and cons through the rest of his shift and made the pointed decision to ignore the buzz of an incoming text message when he said goodnight to Merrick. He didn't look at his phone until he was home, undressed from the day and fresh out of the shower. If he had any luck at all, Merrick would be home and Bryce would be busy and Holden's return text would go unanswered.

He finally read the message from Bryce, groaning and banging his head into the wall as he processed the words.

BRYCE

Send me your address.

Bold of you to assume I want to see you.

Bryce responded almost immediately.

Of course you do.

Holden did want to see him. Unfortunately.

What are you asking for?

What are you offering?

Wasn't that the question of the hour?

Just a fuck, Bryce.

The response—again—came quickly.

What's your address?

Holden sent it and then turned his phone upside down on the arm of his couch.

It took over an hour for Bryce to get there, a sharp knock on the door announcing the other man's arrival. Holden opened the door and drew in a quick breath. In less than six hours, he'd somehow forgotten how handsome Bryce was, but he was grateful for the separation because without Merrick right beside him, it was easier to see Bryce as his own person.

"I made it," Bryce said, leaning against the door frame.

"What did you tell your brother?"

Holden stepped out of the way to let Bryce inside, then closed and locked the door behind him. Bryce looked down at the rack of sneakers beside the door and toed off his own shoes, kicking them toward the wall before grinning up at Holden.

"I told him I was going out to get laid."

"Jesus."

"What?" Bryce laughed. "It's the truth."

"I know, but—"

"He's never going to think it's with you." Bryce reached

out and tugged the hem of Holden's shirt. "Why would it be?"

"Why wouldn't it be?"

Bryce made a thoughtful sound in the back of his throat, and Holden headed back for the couch. He hadn't put too much forethought into the night, but he did bring a bottle of lube and some condoms out from the bedroom just in case things got hot and heavy in the living room. Not that it was a bedroom, necessarily. Holden had a studio apartment, but it was a big one with enough separation in the space he could have a separate living and sleeping area. He had a room divider up to block the bed from the rest of the apartment, but in the heat of the moment, any distance to travel would have probably been too far.

Either way, Bryce ignored his question, sinking down onto the couch like it was *his* couch in *his* living room in *his* apartment. He spread his arms out across the back and smiled at up Holden.

"So," Bryce said. "What's up?"

Holden rubbed the back of his neck and chuckled, sitting down on the couch beside Bryce. "You tell me."

"Maybe we can play a game," Bryce suggested.

"And what's that?"

"You tell me what to do and I'll do it."

Holden bit his tongue between the sharp edges of his canine teeth, swallowing down the flare of arousal that kindled to life in his belly at the very simple and very straightforward offer.

"Get on your knees," he said, spreading his legs a little wider than his usual stance.

Bryce made a happy sound in the back of this throat and did exactly what he'd been told, situating himself between Holden's knees and smiling up at him, hands resting against the top of his thighs. "What now?"

There were two ways he could take this, Holden thought.

He could also be direct or he could take the long way 'round to what they both wanted. He wasn't sure if one or the other was necessarily better, but he was curious to know how far he could push Bryce before it was too far. Holden also very much enjoyed the sight of the other man on his knees, cheeks just on the pink side of normal.

"Take your cock out," he said.

"Mine?" Bryce arched a brow, but reached down and undid the fly of his jeans and pulled his dick out of his pants. He was half-hard, not terribly long, but thick. Precum shined against his crown, and he swiped the moisture away with his thumb before turning his attention back to Holden. "What now? Do you want me to touch myself?"

"No," Holden answered. "I want you to tell me how far is too far."

Bryce bit his lips between his teeth, entire body swaying forward. "I'll try anything twice," he said. "But probably nothing too out of the ordinary tonight."

"What's ordinary for you?"

"Sucking and fucking," he said with a laugh.

Holden gestured toward Bryce's slowly thickening cock. "Do you fuck with that thing?"

Bryce reached down and stroked himself, a long, over-handed tug from root to tip that had him throwing his head back with what Holden assumed had to be a deliberately wanton whimper.

"If you ask nicely."

Holden traced his tongue across the front of his teeth and palmed himself. "What if I don't?"

Bryce laughed at that, a low chuckle that turned into a rich and deep sound. He gave another tug down the length of his cock that looked good enough it had Holden reaching into his pants and making a fist around his own shaft.

"The answer is definitely still a yes." Bryce's stare drifted down Holden's body and he raised a suggestive eyebrow when he reached Holden's lap. "How's the saying go? If you show me yours, I'll show you mine?"

"I've already seen yours."

"Show me," Bryce said quickly, almost a demand if it hadn't sounded so desperate.

Holden was feeling generous, and he obliged Bryce, pulling his already rock-hard cock free from behind the waistband of his black joggers. Bryce's eyes went wide as he watched Holden stroke himself.

"Do you fuck with *that* thing?" Bryce asked.

"Well and often," Holden promised. "Why don't you come a little closer and put it in your mouth?"

Bryce came without needing to be told twice, ignoring his own cock to balance himself against Holden's thighs. He did exactly as he'd been told, taking the head of Holden's cock into his mouth...and not doing anything more. Holden laughed, tangling his fingers into Bryce's dark hair and holding him steady.

"Now suck," he said.

This was well within the limits of whatever vanilla-flavored role play the two of them had actually stumbled into, and Holden would be damned if Bryce didn't take instructions like a champ. The man knew how to suck dick, and he also knew how to follow instructions, because while he had started to suck on Holden's dick, he hadn't taken any more than the tip into his mouth.

"Harder," Holden coaxed, curling the fingers of his other hand around Bryce's shoulder. He lifted his hips off the couch, thrusting another inch into Bryce's mouth. "Deeper."

Bryce made a pleased sound and promptly took Holden's slightly above-average shaft straight down to the root. Holden's eyes rolled back and he held Bryce's head in his lap, giving a few rough thrusts up, right into the back of Bryce's throat. Holden lifted his head back toward the tip and then pushed him back down, showing Bryce the pace he wanted the other man to hold. Again, Bryce proved to be a quick learner, making a wet and sloppy mess of Holden's cock in no time.

Holden stretched for the end table and grabbed a condom, tapping the serrated corner of it against Bryce's cheek until he opened his eyes.

"Do you want me to come in your mouth or inside of you?"

Bryce's lashes fluttered and he pushed himself off Holden's cock and wiped his mouth with the back of his hand.

"Inside of me," he answered, taking the condom from Holden and tearing it open with his teeth. He rolled it down Holden's shaft like he'd done the exact motion a thousand times before, then he fought his way out of his own pants and climbed onto Holden's lap.

"Too impatient to wait for orders here," Bryce said.

Holden rucked up Bryce's shirt until he removed it, then skated his hand up Bryce's chest and held him loosely around the throat. Bryce went still with a soft groan, and Holden gave himself an opportunity to take him in for the first time. Bryce had his hands tattooed and most of his arms. He had a few on his chest and some on the tops of his thighs; he was nowhere near covered but the patchwork style of his art was beyond sexy.

"Slow down or you get nothing," Holden warned.

Bryce's entire body trembled. "I'll try," he promised. "But you know me."

Holden, in fact, didn't know Bryce at all, but that didn't mean he wasn't prepared to get intimately acquainted with the man...and hopefully in more ways than one.

In the condom, Holden's cock throbbed. He was beyond ready to be inside of Bryce. All common sense had gone out the window as soon as he felt the hot press of Bryce's tongue against the underside of his dick. This would just have to be something between them, a secret between men who were barely more than strangers but certainly not friends.

Holden reached for the lube and poured a fair amount onto his fingers. He had no wish to stain his couch, but he wanted Bryce to be ready for him. He tapped the outside of Bryce's thigh and he lifted enough for Holden to reach between them, past Bryce's cock and his heavy balls. Wet fingers sought out Bryce's hole, and he lifted his junk out of the way to make room for Holden's hand.

He pushed one slick finger in and, soon after, another.

"Open yourself up," he whispered. "Show me what you're going to do to my cock once I decide you've earned the right to ride it."

CHAPTER 4

Bryce

HOLDEN HAD long and talented fingers, but his mouth was the problem. For someone who hardly said five words in the course of normal conversation, he seemed to have much more to say when his dick was hard. Bryce, on the other hand, with three fingers up his ass, was admittedly at a loss.

Bryce rode Holden's hand, but the angle was wrong and the stretch was nowhere near enough. He wanted more. He wanted Holden's cock.

"I need more," Bryce managed to admit.

"Another finger?"

Bryce laughed, but it was weak. "I want your cock."

"Where?" Holden asked, but even as the word left his mouth, he eased his hand out of Bryce's body and made a loose grip around his shaft.

"I'll ride it." Bryce shifted his weight until the latex-covered tip of Holden's cock was pressed against his still gaping hole. He should have waited for Holden to lift up, to thrust into him, something…but he was greedy and impatient and he was so fucking horny.

He sank down and took the whole thick length of Holden's cock in one go. It might have been ambitious. His head fell back and a tremor tore through his entire body. Holden shivered and settled his hand around Bryce's hips, steadying him on his lap.

"Wait," Holden rasped. "Wait."

"You're so fucking thick."

Holden huffed out a breath.

"You're so hard, fuck." Bryce's head fell forward, forehead pressing against Holden's while both men took the time they needed to collect themselves before getting going.

"Jesus, you're tight. You're strangling my dick."

"I want you to come," Bryce said, and it was the truth.

He wanted Holden to fuck him for the whole night, but he was equally desperate for Holden to come inside of him. To know what it felt like when Holden's cock thickened and swelled before bursting.

"If you want it," Holden gritted out, "take it."

Bryce fought through another full-body shudder and then he started to move. Slow at first, because his brain was misfiring, his limbs quaking. When Holden reached down and began to stroke Bryce's cock, it didn't make things better or easier. Bryce angled himself backward with one hand braced against Holden's slender thigh, the other curled around Holden's quickly jerking wrist. He balanced himself as much as he could manage considering he was certain they'd transported to an entirely different plane of existence, then he really got going.

If there was one thing Bryce knew, it was how to fuck. Fucking had gotten him in plenty of trouble back home, and it was one of the main reasons Merrick had been so eager to get him to Los Angeles. Bryce had a taste for danger, for the forbidden. It was how he'd ended up with a busted nose in high school (from blowing the captain of the varsity football team—after he asked for it) and also how he'd gotten thrown out of his favorite bar for jerking off the manager after hours—at the manager's request. He would try almost anything twice, and fucking his brother's co-worker felt tame in comparison to some of the things he'd tried in the past.

That wasn't why he found himself naked and sweating on Holden's lap, though. He sincerely found the other man attractive, especially now. With his bleached hair falling into his eyes and his mouth hanging open while Bryce rode him like a bull, Holden was even prettier during sex than he was sitting at a picnic table in the afternoon sun.

That was most likely going to be a problem for Bryce, but he would deal with it later. He'd been honest with Merrick about going out to get laid, but he didn't want to be gone too long. He didn't want to go back to his brother's house and have to answer questions about where exactly he'd been, or worse…with whom.

"I wish you could see yourself," Holden murmured, skating his hands up Bryce's ribs and yanking his mind right back into the present moment. Pleasure slammed into him full speed and Bryce shuddered, forehead falling against Holden's.

"Do I look good?" he managed to ask with a weak laugh. "I feel like I'm going to come so hard I'll never be able to do it again."

That was the truth, not an exaggeration. Holden's hands were good for more than tattooing, and they played Bryce's body like a fucking fiddle.

"That would be a waste."

It was getting hard for him to keep a steady pace, and he was about to ask Holden to take over when the other man caught on.

"Hold on," he said, wrapping one arm around Bryce's back and pressing the other into the couch cushion.

Bryce looped his arms around Holden's neck, and when Holden stood, he hooked his legs around the other man's waist. Holden was slender, but stronger than he looked. He picked Bryce up with ease, even if it meant Bryce sank down and took another inch of Holden's cock up his ass.

Holden carried him around an accordion room divider and threw him down onto a soft and unmade bed. There were pillows everywhere, a mess of blankets, but if Holden cared about order, he didn't show it. Bryce's back hit the sheets and Holden folded him in half, slamming the full length of his cock into Bryce with one quick thrust.

Bryce's eyes rolled back and he fisted the sheets, spreading himself open for Holden to make a meal of. Holden fucked him hard and fast, his face buried in the crook of Bryce's neck the whole time. Bryce grabbed Holden's hair and whimpered, his cock smashed between their stomachs as Holden's pace quickly turned frantic.

"Come inside of me," Bryce whispered, hating there was a condom between them but appreciating the necessity of it for their first time.

"You want that?" Holden nipped at his earlobe.

"Next time," he managed to rasp. "Pretend."

Holden hummed his understanding and flattened his hand against the top of Bryce's head, using it as leverage to thrust harder and deeper into his body.

"I'm going to come so deep inside of you that you'll feel me for a week. My cum is going to be so far up in your asshole it will take days to come out."

Bryce trembled, eyes rolling back.

Fuck, he wanted that.

He really wanted that.

Shoving his hand between their bodies, he took his own dick into his hand and started to stroke, but Holden smacked his arm out of the way, pinned his wrist to the bed.

"No," he said simply.

Bryce made an embarrassing sound, but he wasn't sure if it was from pleasure or embarrassment. He was so horny for this man. Once would certainly not be enough, but turning his brother's co-worker into a secret fuck buddy was going to be a logistical ni—

His brain powered down mid-thought when Holden's mouth touched his.

It was barely a kiss. A dusting of lips, at most.

A question that Bryce answered with parted lips and a searching tongue. As soon as Holden closed that space and slanted their mouths together, it was over for them both. Holden's pace stuttered and his fingers dug hard into Bryce's hair. His hips slammed into Bryce with more force and intent, and with one violent quake, his entire body went still.

"Oh, fuck," Holden whispered. He dropped his head onto the sheets, breath ghosting hot and fast against Bryce's ear.

"Holden."

"So deep. I'm so..." The words died off, but they weren't necessary to begin with.

His cock thickened and pulsed, shooting what Bryce imagined to be an endless stream of cum into his asshole... into the condom.

What a waste.

What a fucking...

Holden pulled out, and Bryce arched off the bed, angry at the loss. He screwed his eyes shut and imagined Holden's cum inside of him, deep and permeating. God, he wanted that. He'd get tested, he'd stop fucking other people, he'd do whatever it took to get Holden raw inside of him.

But, again, Holden shut his brain up entirely. He moved quickly down Bryce's body, took Bryce's hard cock into his mouth and sucked like his life depended on it. Bryce fisted his hair and flew off the bed, fucking his hips against Holden's mouth for less than ten seconds before his orgasm slammed into him.

"Coming," was the only warning he could manage.

He expected Holden to pull off him, to switch to his hand, but he didn't. He sucked and sucked and Bryce shot his load onto Holden's tongue until the pleasure was too much. Holden moved again, this time lower. He sealed his mouth around Bryce's still tender asshole and kissed him there. He speared his tongue into Bryce's hole, and Bryce went limp on the bed. He let go of Holden's hair, let go of his sheets. Every bone left his body as Holden spit and kissed Bryce's own cum into his asshole.

Holden crawled back up his body, the drag of his clothes against Bryce's skin an aphrodisiac in and of itself. Bryce still couldn't open his eyes, and he didn't dare. Especially not when Holden reached down and touched his fingertips against Bryce's hole and smeared his cum around like it was lube. The two of them stayed like that, panting and sweaty, tangled together until Bryce found the strength to open his eyes, to unclench his jaw.

"Just so you know," Holden whispered into his ear, lifting his hand to show Bryce the sticky white mess on his fingertips. "And not that I mind, but a breeding kink isn't a normal part of sucking and fucking."

He managed a laugh that sounded a lot more like a breathy exhale than anything else. "It was just talk, but..."

"Don't try to explain away the things you like." Holden returned his hand to between Bryce's ass cheeks and eased one finger into him. It was nothing compared to the three from earlier, from the punishing stretch of Holden's erect cock. "Am I right, though? Is that what it is?"

"Not in a *I want you to get me pregnant* kind of way," he admitted out loud for what might have been the first time ever. "Just in a...I don't know."

"Use your words."

"Oh." Bryce turned his face to the side, shoved some of Holden's hair off his forehead. "Now you want me to talk?"

Holden grinned and kissed Bryce's chin.

"I just like the idea of being filled with cum," he finally said. "I don't know if there's a name for it."

"Doesn't matter if there is." Holden rolled onto his back and unrolled the condom off his cock. He tied it off and dropped it onto the floor. "You can like what you like without needing to put a name to it."

"And what do you like?"

Holden answered that with a thoughtful noise, batting Bryce's leg up so his hole was more exposed. "I think I definitely enjoy seeing you with cum leaking out of your asshole."

Bryce dropped his leg.

"And I also like when you shut up."

"I like when you talk," Bryce said back quietly.

Holden licked his lower lip, light blue eyes searching Bryce's face for...something. He couldn't be sure, but Bryce imagined it was something like honesty. Before Holden could say anything else, Bryce sat upright, ignoring the head rush.

"I should go," he said.

"Yeah," Holden agreed. "Probably."

Together they climbed out of Holden's bed and shuffled back into the living room. Bryce got dressed, pausing after putting his underwear back on. His own cum was smeared around his asshole and it was hot, but nowhere near enough.

"Can we do this again?" he asked, feeling bold, feeling hopeful.

"I think that's a bad idea," Holden answered. "So, probably yes."

CHAPTER 5
Holden

BRYCE LEFT and Holden sat down on the floor with his back against the door, his legs bent, and his forehead pressed against his knees. What the fuck had he just done and why had it been so fucking hot?

He sat there for at least twenty minutes, alternating between staring up at the ceiling and staring at the wall before remembering he was too old to sit on the floor that long. Holden got up and threw the condom away, then collapsed on his couch with a groan. The whole encounter with Bryce had been hotter than he'd expected. Sure, he'd found Merrick's brother attractive, and he knew from the flirting at lunch the two of them had been working toward fucking. It was the state of the fucking he hadn't expected, was all.

His phone vibrated and he knew without looking it was a message from Bryce, but he pulled it out anyway to read the contents.

It was a picture, Bryce with a tired smile and flushed cheeks, head resting on a pillow with his arm folded back behind his head.

BRYCE

Not that you asked, but I got home safe.

Can we do that again sometime?

Like immediately?

You can't even shut up over text message, can you?

Bryce sent him the "Sssh" emoji, and Holden rolled his eyes.

I felt like I talked less at your house.

Don't you agree?

Yeah

And you…you talked a bit more.

Yeah

Can I come back over tomorrow?

Holden had no real reason why that would be a bad idea, at least, no reason short of all the reasons. The big reason, the main reason—Bryce was Merrick's brother. Merrick was his co-worker. He spent four days a week with less than twenty feet between them. If something went south between him and Bryce, Merrick would certainly hear about it and Holden didn't want things at work to get weird. He liked his job, he liked the shop, and more importantly, he liked his boss. Riggs was a good man, quiet, but not as quiet as Holden. Riggs was reserved where Holden was standoffish, but he was smart and he was an amazing artist. Holden didn't want to do anything to mess up his spot at the shop.

I don't know

Come on. That was hot.

I can't believe you…fuck.

That was unfair, because Holden's curiosity was piqued.

Can't believe I what?

I wanted to have cum inside of me and you
made it happen.

A sharp heat sparked to life in Holden's balls, and he swallowed hard, trying to fight the arousal that kindled to life inside of him at the memory. He had no idea what had come over him with Bryce. Not only did he play into what was obviously a breeding kink, but he'd eaten Bryce's ass and put Bryce's own cum inside of him to help him feel some of that pleasure he'd been after. Holden hadn't thought much about it at the time. The move seemed like something they'd both enjoy, and apparently that choice had paid off.

How deep does that fantasy go for you?

I don't know about having this conversation
over text

Do you have headphones?

He regretted the question as soon as he sent it, but he regretted it more thirty seconds later when his phone rang, Bryce's name flashing across his screen. It was a FaceTime call and he answered it, shoving his hair out of his eyes when Bryce's face filled the screen.

"Where are you?" Holden asked, the background different from the bed Bryce had sent him a picture from.

Bryce angled the phone toward the shower, water

streaming down, then to a closed bathroom door and back to himself.

"Running interference," he said softly.

This was such a bad idea.

"Is your brother awake?"

"He's drawing in the living room. I don't think he would have heard me in the guest room, but I didn't want to risk it."

"Probably better."

Bryce adjusted one of his earbuds and gave a little wiggle.

"Are you sitting on the toilet?" Holden asked.

"The lid is closed."

Holden nodded, then asked again, "How deep does the fantasy go, Bryce?"

"Probably about as deep as the need to hear you moan my name into my ear when you come," Bryce admitted. "Which as of two seconds ago is extraordinarily deep."

Holden scoffed, shaking his head. "That's dramatic."

"It's true."

"Be honest," Holden said.

Bryce's playful smile turned almost somber, his stare working across Holden's face before he answered, "Pretty deep, I think."

Holden wouldn't consider himself kinky, but he also had never considered himself *not* kinky. Sex for him had always been something exploratory and fun, and if that came with spanking or role playing or handcuffs, then that was the law of the land. He'd never really felt dominant or submissive or anything like that, but sometimes the idea of being one or the other was appealing to him. With Bryce, for example, he did enjoy telling him what to do.

And he liked when Bryce did it.

But Bryce could flirt aggressively, and he had done so in the shop, and Holden liked that too.

"Do you feel comfortable telling me?"

Bryce scrubbed a hand down his face and gave a slight shake of his head. "Try again."

"Tell me," Holden said.

Bryce swallowed audibly, and that time, he nodded. "It's not like I want to get pregnant. I don't...don't need to have that sort of talk."

Holden bit his tongue to stop himself from interrupting, from supposing, from guessing.

"But I do like the talk of it, of being filled," Bryce whispered, stare flickering between the phone and the door across from him. "I liked how you tried to make that happen tonight."

Eating ass was not a hardship; neither was filling a hole with cum. It had been quite a while since Holden had taken anyone raw and there was no real reason for him to do that with Bryce, and yet...

"If you get tested," he said, "If we both do."

"Would you?"

"Get tested?" he asked.

"Come inside of me." Bryce paused, licked his lips.

"Yeah," Holden rasped. "Yes."

Just thinking about it made him painfully hard, and he reached down to adjust himself, but Bryce noticed the movement and his earlier curious smile flashed back to life.

"Oh, you like the idea of it?" he teased.

"I also like the idea of coming in your throat," he shot back.

"I think I just..." Bryce went quiet.

"Tell me."

"I'd like that too," he said. "In me, on me...I like all of it."

Holden's muscles clenched, and he nodded. "I'll make a note."

"What about you?" Bryce asked. "What do you like?"

There wasn't much Holden didn't like when it came to

sex. Bryce had been right earlier to call out how much he talked in the moment. Sex was a safe space for him.

"I like the idea of coming inside of you until you're bursting with it," he admitted, and it was true.

"A pleaser, then."

"I also like the idea of taping your mouth shut so you can't talk."

Bryce worried his lower lip. "Would you come in my mouth first?"

Holden's reaction was visceral—a full body tremor that rocked through every muscle so violently he had no choice but to physically feel each twitch and wait until it passed.

"That looks like a yes," Byrce murmured.

Holden reached into his pants and grabbed his cock, stroking his length a couple of times to try and ease back some of his arousal. His touch had the opposite effect, and his hand didn't stop moving.

"That's definitely a yes," Bryce said. "Show me. Let me watch."

Holden propped the phone on his coffee table with the screen angled up toward the couch. He needed both hands, one to reach into his pants and cradle his balls, the other to continue the overhanded assault on his cock. Bryce stayed quiet and attentive while Holden jerked off. The silence undoubtedly gave them both time to imagine their ideal scenarios with the other.

While he held his sac, Holden thought about coming in Bryce's mouth, against his teeth, then gagging him into silence. He didn't know if he would want to use underwear or a gag or tape, but as his mind cycled through the options, he settled on Bryce's underwear, which in that fantasy were dark and soaked with precum. Once Bryce was choking on cum and quiet, Holden would get himself hard again. He would make Bryce watch, or better yet, he would make Bryce do it for him. Once ready, he would fuck Bryce, he would come inside of him, and he wouldn't stop.

Holden was getting older, but he had stamina. He would figure out how to find another orgasm, to find more cum. He would fuck Bryce until he was leaking. He would make Bryce reach between his legs and feel how swollen his hole was. He would have Bryce push the cum back into his body so he didn't lose it so soon after earning it.

In the end, it was the way Bryce looked in Holden's head that sent him over the edge. Yes, Bryce was right there on the phone, looking as delicious as he had at the house, but Holden imagined him sweaty and flushed, desperate and moaning. The Bryce in his brain was in another galaxy for how far gone on pleasure he was and Holden was right there behind him.

He came fast and hard, thick ropes of cum shooting up his stomach and his chest. On the phone, Bryce whimpered, and Holden looked down in time to see Bryce's arm flying off screen for a handful of seconds before going still. Bryce bit his lips hard and threw his head back. Holden's cock was still spurting when he watched Bryce paint the underside of his chin with his own release.

The two of them didn't say anything for a long while after that. They looked at each other, though, stares locked while they caught their breath. Eventually, Bryce smiled at him, a quiet laugh filtering out of the phone and straight into Holden's ears.

"I'm really glad I met you," Bryce said.

Holden groaned, scratching the back of his neck.

A sharp bang through the phone startled them both, and then Merrick's voice rang out, "You're using all my hot water!"

"Fuck off!" Bryce shouted back.

The interruption might as well have been a bucket of cold water over the top of Holden's head. He tucked his dick back into his pants and grabbed his phone. He knew getting involved with Bryce in any capacity was a bad idea, but he wasn't sure he could say no. The attraction between them was incendiary, and that was maybe part of the problem. Or part of the appeal.

"Your brother can't know," Holden said simply.

"I know. But I'm not going to let him stop me from having this."

Holden tapped his finger and thumb together, cum spider-webbing across his knuckles. There was something heady in being wanted, he realized. Not just in being the one doing the wanting.

Bryce wanted him.

For whatever reason, maybe only because he was nice to look at and Bryce wasn't supposed to be looking at him.

Maybe that was enough for now.

On the other end of the call, Bryce set his phone on the vanity and stripped out of his clothes. He didn't put his head-phones back in, but he angled his head toward the shower and Holden understood.

He nodded.

Bryce mouthed the word *tomorrow*, and then the screen went black as the call disconnected.

Holden's home screen wallpaper was a drawing he'd done a few weeks before, nothing fancy, just a yellow rose with thick petals and a coral swirl in the background. It had reminded him of the song he'd been listening to on his way home from work and he'd wanted to remember the feeling of having his windows down with the warm summer air blowing through his hair.

Sometimes, it felt like anything was possible.

Sometimes, it felt like Bryce could be possible.

CHAPTER 6

Bryce

WHEN BRYCE WOKE up the next morning, Merrick was already awake. He found his brother in the kitchen, leaning against the counter and frowning down at his sketchbook.

"Morning," Bryce mumbled, still half asleep.

Merrick pulled a coffee mug down from a cabinet and set it in front of the coffee pot before stepping out of the way for Bryce to fill it himself.

"Did you have a good night last night?" Merrick asked.

Good would have been an understatement. The time he spent with Holden had been off the charts and their phone call had been something else entirely. After they'd gotten off the phone, Bryce had actually showered. He'd avoided Merrick, managed to get himself into bed, and fell asleep before his head hit the pillow. He woke in the morning with a pleasurable ache between his legs and a pounding urgency to find a clinic offering same-day test results.

He shivered and wiped some sleep from the corner of his eye. "I did."

"What's his name?" Merrick asked.

"Does it matter?"

"I don't know. Are you going to see him again?"

Obviously.

"At least once," he said, because it was the truth. He and Holden had plans for another round and he would see Holden whenever he went to Ink and Ember, but he didn't think any of that meant anything. Whatever was happening between them was just sex, or if it wasn't, it needed to be.

"When?"

"Tonight." Bryce rested his elbows on the counter and looked down at the dragon his brother had been sketching. "What about you? Are you seeing anyone?"

Merrick sniffed and flipped the cover on his sketchbook closed. "No."

It was the shortest answer his brother had ever given him about anything.

Bryce turned and leaned against the counter, sipping his coffee without looking directly at Merrick. "Tell me more about that."

"There's nothing to tell."

"You always have something to say."

Merrick cleared his throat and turned around, leaning against the edge of the counter and mirroring Bryce's pose. The two of them held their coffee the same way and stared out the window over the sink. Bryce thought about Holden, and he had no idea what—or who—Merrick was thinking about.

"How was your flight?" Merrick asked instead.

A deflection.

"Short, but it was fine. Had some ginger ale and some of that over-dry trail mix. Flirted with a flight attendant."

"Was she pretty?"

Bryce smiled, thinking about the slender twink.

"He was."

"Have you ever met a person you didn't want to take to bed?"

The question was more an accusation, and Merrick's tone was biting.

"You," he answered. "And please don't pretend like you care about what I do behind closed doors."

"You don't even always close the doors."

"You weren't supposed to be home until eight!"

His brother snorted a laugh in the back of his throat, shaking his head.

Bryce had struggled trying to get the right kind of attention growing up. Merrick had always been such a personality, in and out of their house, it was as if Bryce was born with shoes to fill. There was no corner of his life where he wasn't compared to his older brother. And he loved Merrick, he really did, but he didn't want to be like him and that was a hard pill for everyone around them to swallow.

Merrick was good at art, better than good, obviously. Bryce still drew oval-shaped suns in the corners of the page. Merrick had always been a good student, straight A's in everything, where Bryce had to work for C's. Merrick's gift for conversation had made him the center of attention while Bryce's struggle to be heard over the chatter of his brother made him a troublemaker...a distraction. But when the two of them were alone together, Bryce saw a mirror of himself and he didn't understand why everything that came so readily to Merrick had been so difficult for him.

It was one of the big reasons he'd wanted to leave home. Bryce was desperate to be somewhere people could know him as himself, not as Merrick's brother. So, of course, the first thing he did was go find himself a man who knew him as the latter. Even if he did have plans to see Holden again, the next time needed to be the last time. Bryce hadn't moved to LA to stay in his brother's shadow, and he certainly didn't want to start out there.

"So, what's your plan then?" Merrick asked. "You can stay

here as long as you need. Until you can get a job and get some money saved."

"I have money saved."

"Things are different here."

"I'm not a child," he snapped. "I know LA is expensive. I know it's a hard city."

Merrick exhaled, blowing the breath into his coffee before taking a drink. "What do you think you want to do?"

"I was going to see if I could find a bartending gig or something," he said. "I really don't want to start serving again—"

"Too many actors already waiting tables anyway," Merrick interrupted.

Bryce snorted. "And I'll start looking for apartments tomorrow."

"You don't have to."

"I know."

He wanted to. He loved his brother, he did. But he was using Merrick as a steppingstone. A helping hand to get out of St. Jack's Bay and settled somewhere new.

"Do you work today?" Bryce asked.

Merrick nodded and turned his attention back to his sketchbook, focusing again on the unfinished dragon he'd been stabbing his pencil at when Bryce had woken up.

"Tell me about it," Bryce said, knowing how to use his brother's chatter as a tool to change the mood when he wanted to.

"This dragon at two," he said, sliding the drawing toward Bryce. It was a beautiful Japanese-style thing, clearly designed for a forearm. Bryce might not be an artist himself, but because of Merrick he'd grown up around enough of them to know the basics of how tattoos wrapped around the body. He had a few of his own, most done by his brother and some done by his brother's friends. He was nowhere near as inked as Merrick, and both of them had much more open skin than Holden, who was covered pretty much from his throat to his ankles.

Bryce wanted to see him naked.

Shit.

"I meant tell me about the shop. About your life here."

"Riggs is a good boss," Merrick explained. "An amazing artist. He has a boyfriend who comes around a lot named Smith. He's young, but still older than you."

Bryce rolled his eyes.

"He opened the shop after his husband died. He just hired me and Holden not too long ago."

"I remember," Bryce said.

"It's small and it's quiet—"

"You've never been quiet a day in your life."

Merrick grinned. "Holden tells me that at least once a day."

Bryce should have known asking about work would derail the conversation into dangerous territory. He focused himself on Merrick's sketchbook, flipping through the pages to see what else his brother had been working on. It was easy to tell which drawings were for clients and which had been for himself. Merrick had always been fascinated with nature, drawing flowers and birds and trees since he learned to pick up a pencil. At least that was the story their parents always told. Merrick had been drawing since before Bryce had even been born.

Deciding it would invoke more attention if he ignored the topic of Holden completely, Bryce took a drink of coffee and asked, "What's his deal, anyway?"

The question was twofold. He did want to know about the other man, but he wanted to keep his brother off his tail too.

"He's cranky," Merrick said. "Quiet. He keeps to himself."

"Everyone is quiet when you're around."

"Not you."

Bryce didn't tell his brother that was from necessity. Instead he took another drink of his coffee.

"How was your little lunch adventure yesterday?" Merrick asked. "He didn't say anything about it when he got back to the shop."

Enlightening, Bryce thought to himself.

"Uneventful," he answered. "He doesn't have much to say."

Unless he's horny, Bryce though, in which case it's nearly impossible to shut him up.

"I don't know what his deal is."

"What do you mean?"

"His deal," Merrick repeated, like saying the same thing again would somehow clarify it.

"Merrick."

"I don't know. He just comes to work, does his job, and leaves. I don't know a single thing about him."

"Have you ever asked?"

"What?" Merrick scoffed at him. "Of course."

Bryce raised a brow, decidedly in disbelief. His brother was kind, but he rarely thought to engage others in the talking parts of his day.

"Is that why you made him take me to eat?" he asked.

"I asked him to take you to eat because you were hungry and directions to the corner store are confusing."

"It was three blocks," Bryce said.

He closed Merrick's sketchbook and looked at his brother, who was staring at him with an uncomfortable kind of intensity.

"What?" he asked.

"Nothing," Merrick answered quickly. He clutched his coffee to his chest and walked out of the kitchen toward the living room.

Bryce topped his mug off before following after his brother and finding him on the couch. He sat down next to

Merrick and stretched his legs out, propping his socked heels on the coffee table. This time, Merrick was the one to match his pose, crossing his legs at the ankle.

"What?" he asked again.

"I think he's lonely," Merrick blurted, and Bryce could have laughed at the absurdity of it.

"Why do you think that?"

"He's just so quiet! I don't think he has any friends. I don't think he has a girlfriend, and I don't think he has any family here. I just…"

"You didn't have any family here until yesterday," Bryce countered. "And if you have a girlfriend, you haven't told me."

"I have friends," his brother argued.

"I'm not saying you don't. I'm just saying it sounds like you don't really know a single thing about him so I'm not sure what your goal is."

"I don't think he has friends and you don't know anyone here," Merrick explained. "I thought the two of you could maybe be friends."

"I'm sure he has friends."

"You don't."

Bryce sighed. When his brother got like this, there was no stopping him. Merrick would get these ideas in his head and convince himself they were real, even if they had no basis in reality. Bryce figured it had to do with Merrick's overactive imagination or something. He'd never been sure.

"I'm fine, Mer. And I'm sure he is too."

"Well, if you wanted to be friends with him—"

"I don't," Bryce said sharply. Maybe too sharply. He forced a smile and shrugged his shoulders. "He probably doesn't want to be friends with me."

"Who wouldn't want to be friends with you?"

Plenty of people, Bryce thought to himself. Everyone who compared him to Merrick and found him lacking, for one.

Everyone who compared him to Merrick and found him worse, for two. He'd never tell his brother that, though. For as much as Merrick stressed him out and hurt his feelings with his talent and his general ability to be perfect at everything, Bryce never wanted Merrick to know how that had impacted the people around them. Nothing bad that had happened to Bryce had ever been Merrick's fault directly. And for as much as his brother annoyed him, he really didn't want Merrick to change.

He just wanted to exist, and he wanted that to be enough.

He wanted to be quiet sometimes and he wanted to breathe, and he didn't want to be compared to someone he'd never wanted to be in the first place.

"I want a new tattoo," he said, stretching his leg out and kicking Merrick in the ankle.

The change of direction in conversation was exactly what the both of them needed. Merrick angled his body toward Bryce and tucked one leg beneath himself, cradling his coffee mug with both hands.

"Oh?" Merrick raised his eyebrows and smiled. "Tell me more. Actually wait, let me get my sketchbook first."

CHAPTER 7

Holden

AT SIX FIFTEEN, Holden got a text message from Bryce. It was a picture of a printout from the clinic giving Bryce a clean bill of health. He'd sent a second message with an eggplant emoji and a string of the splash ones. Holden groaned and turned his phone face down on the counter.

"Everything good?" Merrick asked from his booth.

Holden swallowed down a second groan. "Everything is fine," he said.

Merrick was silent for five blessed seconds before he spoke again, "Do you think you could show my brother around town?"

There was no stopping the groan that time, and Holden rolled his stool as far away from Merrick as he could reach. He, of course, took no issue with the prospect of showing Bryce anything. He took issue with Merrick knowing about it, orchestrating it…directing it. Bryce was his own person, and Merrick's incessant yammering and prodding about his brother had already started to sound like interference. Merrick had spent the whole day talking about his brother, about what Bryce did for fun, what he did for work, how he couldn't draw.

It made Holden feel…he wasn't sure.

Uncomfortable, maybe.

If he wanted to get to know Bryce outside of the bedroom, he wanted to do it on his terms, or on their own terms. He hated the way Merrick spoon-fed everyone within earshot information about a man who wasn't even in the room, coloring their opinions about Bryce before he even had a chance to make his own impressions.

"Isn't he old enough to not need a keeper?" Holden asked.

"He doesn't have any friends here."

"He's been here for thirty hours."

"You know what I mean," Merrick argued, letting off the power on his machine so he could be better heard. He glanced at his client. "My brother just got into town yesterday. He doesn't know anyone."

"I gathered," Merrick's client said, not bothering to even look up from the game on her phone. She shoved the second earbud into her ear, and Holden couldn't stop himself from laughing under his breath about how effective the technique was at shutting Merrick up. Unfortunately, removing herself from the equation meant Merrick only had him and Riggs to talk at, and Riggs was so intensely focused on work, the building could have been on fire and he wouldn't have noticed.

"Just let him settle in a bit before you start to meddle," Holden suggested.

He'd finished with his client just after six and didn't have anything on the books for the rest of the night. He and Bryce hadn't set a specific time, and as the minutes crept on, Holden felt himself getting antsy. He and Bryce had talked about a lot of things, in person and on the phone, and it wasn't that Holden couldn't back up the talk, it was…he'd never had a chance to before.

"If I give you his number, will you text him?" Merrick asked.

"Absolutely not."

There was something to be said as well about the thrill of whatever this thing with Bryce was turning out to be. Holden wasn't ashamed of his bisexuality or of any past—or future—promiscuity, but there was something decidedly exciting about having Bryce as a secret. He wasn't sure if Merrick would be upset to find out Holden was sleeping with his younger brother, but he wasn't sure he wouldn't be. Holden also had no interest in finding out because whatever was happening between him and Bryce was far from serious, and he got the impression Merrick would absolutely try to make it serious.

"He doesn't know anyone here," Merrick repeated.

"He talks as much as you, so I'm sure it won't take him long to make a friend."

Holden typed out a quick message on his phone to let Bryce know he was leaving work. He ignored whatever Merrick said in response to him and instead told the other man goodbye. He knocked elbows with Riggs, then grabbed his stuff and left. On his way to the car, he pulled up a copy of his most recent test results and sent them in a reply text to Bryce.

You're the only person I've been with since these came in.

Bryce responded quickly.

You went a whole week without it? Impressive.

Holden ignored the taunt, appreciating how twice in two days was a dramatic departure from his month-long slump. Bryce didn't even know how long it had been for him. Not that it mattered. He would tell Bryce if he asked. Was that maybe the sort of conversation they should be having considering the roleplaying they were planning to do together?

Holden wasn't sure, but any decent thoughts went out of his brain entirely when he got home and found Bryce already there and waiting, leaning against his front door with his arms folded in front of his chest and his eyes closed.

"Can I help you?" Holden murmured, boxing Bryce in against the door and reaching around him to get his key into the lock.

"I hope so," Bryce said without opening his eyes. He angled his neck upward and Holden pressed a wet kiss against the corded muscle.

The lock disengaged, and the two of them stumbled inside. They both took off their shoes, and Holden kicked the door closed. He dropped his keys on the floor and immediately put his hands on Bryce, who groaned and smashed their bodies, and their mouths, together. God, this man was so fucking hot, so horny, so *ready*.

"I haven't been able to stop thinking about you since I left," Bryce whispered into Holden's mouth while his fingers tugged mindlessly at his shirt.

"Is that so?"

"I've been desperate to get you naked."

Holden hummed, pulling his shirt off and tossing it onto the floor. He walked Bryce backward to his bed, dropping his knee between Bryce's legs when they both went down on top of the sheets. Bryce scooted back, struggling out of his shirt and fighting with the fly on his jeans. Holden batted his hands away and kissed Bryce's chest, then lower and lower. He made Bryce's pants his responsibility, his underwear next, then his socks. All of it discarded on the floor and Bryce naked on his bed, hard and leaking.

"Please let me see you," Bryce begged, jerking his chin toward Holden's belt.

He climbed back off the bed and loosened his pants,

opening them before taking them off. He tugged down the waistband of his black boxer briefs, showing Bryce a nest of dark curls and the base of his thickening shaft.

Bryce cursed under his breath and Holden stroked himself in his underwear, making sure to smear precum across as much of the material as he could manage. He stripped out of his pants and his socks, but crawled back onto the bed with his underwear still in place. He knee-walked up to Bryce's face and rubbed his underwear-covered cock across the man's chin, grunting in pleasure when Bryce's hungry mouth tried to chase after him.

"Settle," Holden warned, tucking the waistband of his underwear behind his cock and balls. He tapped his tip on Bryce's nose before dragging it down toward his lips. "You don't have to be so loud here. I still hear you."

Bryce's response wasn't much more than a stuttered moan and a desperate lift of his hips that sent Holden rocking forward toward his mouth. And fuck, what a mouth it was. Holden fed his cock onto Bryce's waiting tongue, inch by inch by inch, shuddering when he felt teeth, when Bryce had to swallow, exhale through his nose, stretch his jaw to accommodate Holden's girth.

With most of his dick in Bryce's mouth, Holden released the base of his shaft and put both of his hands into Bryce's hair, smoothing it away from his face. He traced his fingertips over Bryce's eyebrows and down, brushing tears from the corners of his eyes before reaching around to the back of his head and holding him down to the bed.

"You want me to fuck your face?" he asked.

Bryce nodded, pupils dilated and nostrils flaring.

"If you want me to stop anything, tell me to stop," Holden said. "If your mouth is full, smack me."

With a mouthful of cock, Bryce smiled.

Holden shut him up, thrusting into the back of his throat until Bryce choked.

"God, you're close to perfect when you're quiet," Holden murmured, holding Bryce to the bed by his hair and starting a pace so slow it felt a lot like torture.

Bryce was probably very near perfect when he wasn't quiet, but that wasn't part of whatever little roleplay Holden had found himself in that night. Either way, he liked it. He liked the way Bryce's bare chest felt beneath him, the way his hot and wet mouth gurgled as he tried to suck Holden's cock. He also liked the promise of what was to come later.

Holden lost himself in Bryce's mouth, in Bryce's sounds, in his silence. He couldn't remember the last time he'd been so desperate for another person, and the tight hole of Bryce's mouth might be his new favorite place. Needing to get deeper, he pulled out long enough to climb off the bed, to haul Bryce onto his knees.

With spit smeared across his chin and his cheeks, Bryce blinked up at him and stuck his tongue out, asking for more without using his words. Holden still had Bryce's hair in his fist. He smacked his cock against Bryce's hollowed-out cheek, then fucked right back into his throat. Bryce sputtered and spit, but he never took his stare off Holden's face.

Holden knew time was going to be his worst enemy in this situation. He wasn't as young as he used to be, and while multiple orgasms in one night were definitely something he was capable of, it wasn't always a sure thing. He either needed no downtime or enough of it, and he quickly realized he was about to have neither of those.

"Don't move," he warned, drawing himself out of Bryce's hungry mouth.

He went to the nightstand, grabbed the lube, and shoved it into Bryce's hand.

"Get yourself ready," he said, sliding back into the heat of his still open mouth. Bryce moved and rearranged himself, groaning so deep once he got his fingers into himself it vibrated Holden's cock.

"I can't wait to come inside of you from every possible entrance. Fill you up with it until you're leaking."

Bryce whimpered, and Holden gritted his molars together. He was right on the edge, but he needed Bryce to be a little more prepped before he took him that way. With reluctance, he eased himself out, dragging his dick across the tip of Bryce's tongue. After a few agonizing minutes of Holden staring at the ceiling because the absolute wanton lust on Bryce's face was far too much for him to survive, Bryce made a plaintive little sound that drew Holden's attention back.

"I know," he whispered, fighting the way his eyes wanted to roll back. "You're so fucking hungry for it. Aren't you?"

Bryce nodded, spreading his mouth as wide as he could manage.

Holden pulled out enough that he could get his hand around his dick and three strokes later, it was over. His orgasm hit him like a freight train and a violent burst of cum landed hot and white against Bryce's pink tongue. Fuck, it was a lot of cum. Jet after jet of it landed on Bryce's tongue, a stray drop against the corner of his mouth.

Bryce reached down with his slippery fingers and started to stroke himself, and Holden fought his way out of his underwear, balling up the wet mess and shoving it as deep as he could get it into Bryce's mouth. He gagged more around that than Holden's cock, his eyes going wide as he got used to the stretch.

"Finally," Holden murmured, admiring all the spit on his still pulsating shaft. "Now I can fuck you for real."

CHAPTER 8

Bryce

BRYCE WAS VERY close to coming on the spot and untouched. Between the wet underwear stretching his jaw open and the cum streaking down his tongue into the back of his throat, he didn't think he'd ever been happier. That was, at least, until Holden hauled him onto the bed, put him on all fours, and then shoved that thick cock right up his ass. Bryce tried to cry out, but the sound of it was muffled by the makeshift gag. He tried to suck in a breath, but inhaling forced cum too far into his throat. He couldn't taste it. He wanted to taste it.

"Stop rushing," Holden coaxed, pressing the heel of his palm between Bryce's shoulder blades until he arched his back and rested his chest against the mattress.

Bryce tried to take the very sexy advice to heart. His lashes fluttered closed and he focused on breathing through his nose. He didn't have to do anything there. There was nothing to say. The sound of Holden's skin slapping against his was almost enough to lull him into a meditative state, and he probably would have, were it not for the persistent drag of Holden's cock against his prostate…and deeper.

He had no idea how Holden was still going, but he certainly wasn't interested in arguing about it. Instead, Bryce let the pleasure in his body become the only thing that mattered, the rough press of Holden's fingers against his skin. Time passed, or maybe it stopped, Bryce wasn't sure. He didn't notice anything at all until a sharp wave of arousal crashed against him with enough force to shove him over the edge and headfirst into an orgasm that had him seeing stars.

There was no stopping the noise then, the frantic crying and gagging and choking. He scrabbled against the sheets for purchase, and all the while Holden slammed into him from behind. Relentless.

"I'm so close," Holden murmured, his fingers certainly digging bruises into Bryce's hips. "Want to see your face when I pump you full of cum."

And then Bryce was on his back, one leg in the air, his calf propped on Holden's shoulder as Holden thrust into him again. Holden was a mess, sweaty and flushed, the muscles on his stomach and chest rippling with every move. Holden pushed some more of his underwear into Bryce's mouth, sealing his lips around the corners to make sure no spit—or sound—came out.

"Yeah," Holden said, eyes searching Bryce's face. "I know."

Bryce wasn't sure what Holden meant, but he had ideas.

"I'm going to come so fucking hard inside of you," Holden promised. "So much cum it's going to spill out of you because your body can't hold it all."

Bryce's eyes rolled back, and he nodded eagerly.

"You have to help, though," Holden went on, dirty talk spilling out of him like the faucet he wanted to turn Bryce into. "You have to milk it out of me, yeah? Make sure you take every drop I've made for you. Every drop of cum in my balls needs to be in your fucking guts before we're done here. Right?"

Bryce's cock pulsed.

"That's what you want, and that's what I'm going to give you." Holden's pace faltered. He was close. "You don't even have to ask for it. I know what you want, right? I know what you need."

If Bryce hadn't just finished, that would have been the line that did it for him. He hooked his hand around the back of Holden's neck and pulled their faces together until they were forehead to forehead. He wanted to kiss Holden, he was desperate for it, but Holden's underwear was still in his mouth, Holden's cum in his throat.

"Here it comes," Holden whispered against Bryce's stretched and trembling upper lip. Another violent slam of Holden's hips and then both of them were still.

Bryce *could* feel it. The hot, pulsing stretch as Holden came inside of him. It was perfect, better than he had imagined it to be. Holden came and came and came, and Bryce imagined it as he'd said. Body so full of cum that it would spill out of him, leak all over his thighs and the bed. There was so much cum, Bryce wouldn't be able to keep all of it inside of him.

Fuck, Bryce wanted more of it.

A weak drop of pleasure pooled in the slit of his own dick, either leftover or new, he didn't know. Holden reached between their bodies and eased himself out an inch, groaning.

"I'm still coming. Oh, fuck."

Holden withdrew from his body inch by inch, milking himself into Bryce's hole as he went. When the tip of Holden's cock finally popped free, Bryce's body clenched and gaped, chasing after him.

"Settle down," Holden murmured, pressing three fingers against Bryce's hole until the muscles relaxed.

Above him, Holden's chest heaved with every breath. Bryce didn't think he'd taken a full breath since Holden shoved his cock into Bryce's mouth, but he didn't mind. He was in heaven there, on his back with Holden above him,

Holden's cum inside of him. A meteor could have crashed into the apartment and incinerated them both, and Bryce would have been happy for it.

He flexed his fingers against the back of Holden's neck, the two of them still frozen in an extremely vulnerable and intimate pose, and then he waited for the shoe to drop. Waited for Holden to climb off of him, waited for the awkward goodbye that was certain to follow what they'd just done.

What he got instead was a flash of Holden's white smile, a slow pull on the gag in his mouth as Holden used his teeth to extract the gag from Bryce's throat. Holden flung his head to the side and spit the underwear on the ground, rubbing his thumb across Bryce's chin while he worked his jaw closed and tried to ease some of the ache that came with being held open for so long.

And then a kiss.

The softest brush of Holden's lips across his, and then he eased Bryce's leg down, worked his fingers into the tense muscle at Bryce's hip. Holden rolled onto his side, but instead of rolling away, he took Bryce with him so they were both face to face in the bed. He opened his mouth to say thank you, but Holden shook his head, pressed those cum and lube-slick fingers against Bryce's mouth.

"Don't," he said simply. "I know."

Bryce nipped at Holden's fingers, eyes rolling back when he obliged and eased them into Bryce's mouth. There was no force behind it, nothing more than him honoring Bryce's request to taste and suck and bite. It was almost casual, and Bryce grabbed Holden's wrist so he didn't take his hand back. Bryce eased Holden's fingers out as he wanted, swirling his tongue around the nail beds and the knuckles, holding Holden's stare the entire time. Finally, he ended his assault with a kiss, leaving Holden's fingers against the outside of his lips. He let his hand fall away, and Holden didn't move.

Maybe being told to be quiet wasn't always enough.

As much as he wanted the silence, he obviously didn't know how to sit with himself for long enough to enjoy it. He needed Holden's cock in his mouth or a gag or Holden's fingers. Maybe need was too strong of a word, but he very much wanted it.

He enjoyed it.

He craved it.

Holden didn't seem to mind. He kept his hand where Bryce left it, brushing a kiss against his forehead before settling his head onto the pillow. And they stayed like that for so long Bryce lost track of the time, but his eyelids grew heavy and it was hard to keep them open.

"Do you want to stay the night?" Holden asked, voice cracking as he shattered the silence.

Bryce didn't open his eyes, but he managed to nod.

"Do you want me to clean you up?"

He shook his head.

"Do you want some more?" he whispered.

Bryce's heart could have exploded.

"Yes," he whispered.

Holden tapped his hip. "Roll over, other side."

Bryce groaned, but made the flip onto his other side so his back was to Holden's chest. Holden was gentle with him, lifting Bryce's leg to make room, rubbing his half-hard cock against Bryce's soiled asshole until he was all the way hard again. Holden's cock felt swollen and thick as he entered Bryce for the second time, or third depending on how he counted the night. And while the intent of the act was the same as before, the action of it was far from it.

Holden moved inside of him with long, languid thrusts. His sweaty fingers grabbed at Bryce's skin, like he was trying to stop from losing himself which was hilarious because Bryce was already gone. There was no rush in it, no anticipation. This was a different sort of sex entirely, almost tender enough to rock Bryce into a much-needed sleep.

"Do you want to come?" Holden asked softly, teeth cool against Bryce's ear.

He thought about it, because why wouldn't he want to come? But then he decided there was...more to be had here than just chasing after an ending.

"No," he admitted.

Holden growled in his ear and thrust twice more before shuddering and going still. His cock pulsed and spilled into Bryce's body, and Bryce knew there was probably enough cum inside of him now that it would actually overflow and leak out, all over his balls and the base of Holden's still throbbing shaft.

The pleasure of it must have taken Holden too, because he reached around and petted his hand down Bryce's chest before his tattooed fingers splayed upward toward Bryce's throat. Holden pulled their bodies closer, keeping his dick lodged firmly inside of Bryce's hole.

"Rest," Holden told him, and Bryce didn't need to be told twice.

He closed his eyes and promptly fell asleep.

———

Bryce dreamed of indecent things, things that only happened in books he'd read and porn he'd seen on the internet. He woke up later in the night, hard and leaking, Holden's cock barely still inside of him. He moved his arm back, grasping Holden's hip before falling back into dreams.

———

He woke again later to moonlight streaming through the window and an ache in his shoulder from holding Holden's thigh for what had to have been hours. Holden's face was still buried against the back of his neck, Holden's cock hard and wet against his asshole. He didn't mean to wake Holden, but his hips pushed back against the erection his body so urgently wanted.

"Again?" Holden rasped, the sheets rustling as he moved.

"Please."

Holden made an affirmative sound and rolled Bryce onto his stomach. The lube opened, some of it spilling down Bryce's crack, and then the familiar sound of wet skin against wet skin as Holden slicked his cock.

"You're a leaking mess," Holden told him, lining the head of his dick up with Bryce's still tender hole. "I don't even know if there's room for me in here."

Bryce's entire body shivered, and he bit the pillow to stop himself from saying anything back. Holden thrust into him, the wet squelch of his entry enough to wake Bryce's dick up along with the rest of him. Holden fucked him steady and hard, the bed creaking beneath them with every slam of Holden's hips. Holden fucked him for a good five minutes before coming, another hot rush of cum into the deepest parts of him that had Bryce writhing against the sheets.

He arched his back, grabbed Holden's hip, and kept the other man deep inside of him. Holden came hard with a low and rumbling growl that caused gooseflesh to prick up along the back of Bryce's neck.

"I could stay like this for days," Holden said quietly, dusting a kiss against Bryce's warm skin. "Just fucking you and filling you and falling asleep then waking up and doing it all over again."

"Tease," he murmured.

Holden didn't stay inside of him for long after the last orgasm, and Bryce winced at the emptiness. He rolled onto his side to face Holden, whose expression was as unreadable as it had been the day before when they'd met for the first time.

"I'm serious," he said, and Bryce swallowed hard, stunned into silence.

CHAPTER 9

Holden

THE SHEETS WERE A TANGLED and sweaty mess. Bryce was flushed, his hair stuck to his forehead, and Holden could only guess what the insides of his thighs looked like. Holden shoved his hair away from his face and rolled onto his back, covering his eyes with a forearm.

He shouldn't have said that.

But he'd meant it just the same.

After the admission, he'd expected Bryce to have something witty or horny to retort. What he got instead was a sad little whimper and the insistent press of Bryce's body against his. Holden wrapped his arms around him and kissed the top of his head, hating the way it made his chest feel to have Bryce so close. Neither of them said anything for an achingly long time until Bryce finally murmured, "I don't want to go back to my brother's house."

The reminder of Merrick's role in their lives was a rude awakening, dashing any ideas he'd had about keeping Bryce locked in the bedroom all weekend, of tying him to the bed and pumping him full of cum. It was a shame, Holden thought, that Bryce didn't want to role play the whole breeding part of the breeding kink, because for the first time in his life, he saw the appeal of it. The primal rutting and thrusting of it, the need to get as deep as possible, to come more than he ever had before.

"But I don't want to overstay," Bryce said next, and Holden petted his fingers along the side of Bryce's face.

"Please stop talking."

Bryce hummed and went quiet.

Holden closed his eyes. He needed to think, needed to assess the possible options and outcomes for the mess he'd gotten himself into. Fucking Bryce was absolutely supposed to be a one-time thing, maybe two...three at best. He definitely hadn't set out with the intent to like fucking Bryce so much. He'd gone into it pretty sure fucking Bryce would be like fucking anyone else. Maybe there would be a little more sense of adventure because he was Merrick's little brother, but the feelings Holden was having about Bryce didn't reflect any of those earlier plans. If the first option was out the window, he might as well try number two and see what results it would yield.

"Don't move," he said, unfolding himself from Bryce's still trembling body. He'd planned to go get some snacks from the fridge, but seeing Bryce naked and so very messy in bed, Holden didn't feel right leaving him there without covering him up. Unfortunately, he didn't want to put him into a bath either, knowing without asking that Bryce wasn't ready to lose all the cum Holden had so carefully loaded into him.

Trying to meet himself in the middle, he went and grabbed a blanket from the back of the couch and adjusted as much of it over the sheets as he could manage before rolling Bryce back onto the top of it. It wasn't warm, but at least it was dry.

"Are you okay?" Holden asked, tapping his mouth with the side of his first finger.

Bryce opened his mouth and quickly closed it, answering Holden with a nod.

"I'll be right back."

Holden went around the divider, this time into the kitchen. He didn't have a ton of stuff in the fridge. He was a snacker at best, a youngest child who'd grown up with ingredients not food. Holden was used to making do with the things he had available. So he did his best to assemble a plate that looked a lot like rabbit food. He took it and a bottle of water back to the bed, ignoring the way Bryce's eyes went soft at his return.

"You should eat," he suggested, setting the plate beside his leg where Bryce could reach it.

Bryce grabbed a couple of almonds, a slice of cheese, and shoved it all into his mouth with a grateful moan. He chewed, swallowed, then must have realized how hungry he was and devoured the plate before Holden could even get his hands onto it. Holden could get himself more; he didn't mind. He passed Bryce the water, and thankfully he drank slowly without being told.

"Do you want more?" Holden asked.

Bryce's dark eyes scanned Holden's face before he shook his head.

"Let me put this in the sink."

He could have easily left the plate on the nightstand. Bryce hadn't left any crumbs, but he needed space. He needed air. The way Bryce looked at him was dangerous. The way he said so much without ever uttering a word, somehow even worse than when he wouldn't stop talking. Holden set the plate in the sink and braced himself against the edge of the counter, head hanging low between his shoulders.

The right thing to do was send Bryce home.

Get him into a shower—not a bath—and hope it was enough time for the cum to leak out of him. He'd sit on the couch while Bryce got dressed again, and then Holden would delete his number. It would be fine. It would be better. Bryce was handsome and he was smart. He was new to LA. He would find someone far better suited for him than Holden was.

A soft brush of fingertips against the small of his back startled him, and Holden turned with a gasp. Bryce was there, naked and still sweaty, cock limp and swollen against his thigh.

"I was about to come back," Holden explained.

Bryce rolled his eyes, taking the no talking thing very seriously apparently, then he sank to his knees.

"You don't have—"

But Bryce cut him off—silently—by drawing a little spiral in front of his mouth before curling his fingers around Holden's thigh. The gesture was clear. Where Holden had told Bryce to stay quiet, Bryce wanted him to keep talking.

Before Holden could find any argument inside of him, his cock was in Bryce's mouth. He cursed under his breath, flexing his fists at his sides before threading his fingers into Bryce's hair and thrusting gently into his mouth. Holden didn't think he had another orgasm in him, but the wet cavern of Bryce's mouth felt a lot like heaven. As quickly as he had it, it was gone, and Holden looked down to see Bryce smirking up at him, repeating the gesture as when he'd gone to his knees in the first place.

Bryce wanted him to talk.

Holden tightened his grip on Bryce's hair and groaned, giving up what Bryce wanted from him...again.

"You're so fucking good at this," he whispered, eyes hooded while he watched Bryce eagerly suck him. "I would keep my cock here all night if I could. I'd never leave."

Bryce groaned something that sounded like approval, blinking earnestly up at him.

"This is what you're good for, isn't it?" he asked next, giving a gentle tug to Bryce's hair. He angled Bryce's face toward him, wanting to make sure he didn't overstep the boundaries of their little game. "Good for holding my cum, aren't you?"

Bryce's entire body trembled and he swirled his tongue around the tip of Holden's cock. He was almost fully hard by then, even though an orgasm still felt unlikely to him considering how many he'd given Bryce earlier, but he didn't think what they were doing had anything to do with orgasms.

Holden tried to relax into the pleasure of it, the want and the need with none of the expectation. He rested his ass against the counter and pumped his hips lazily into Bryce's hungry and waiting mouth, shivering as arousal coursed through him.

"I want to come in you again," he finally confessed, hating how true it was.

Bryce made a happy sound and Holden shoved as much of his cock into his mouth as he could fit. He held Bryce near the root of his dick, enjoying the way his lips were spread wide, the way tears beaded in the corners of his eyes as he tried not to choke and gag.

There was an orgasm there, he realized.

Not a massive, earth-quaking thing. It was more a tremor that built in the marrow of his bones and vibrated through him, shaking all the need loose from the very deepest parts of him. He came like that, a soft roll up his spine and a fierce heat between his legs as he spilled drops of cum onto Bryce's tongue. Bryce's eyes rolled back and he shuddered, hollowing his cheeks and swallowing down what he'd made for him.

Holden was drunk with pleasure, with power, for the need to convince himself he *could* have this. The option to send Bryce packing no longer existed, at least not yet. Even in the haze of an unexpected orgasm, he knew Bryce would tire of this game eventually. The novelty would wear off, and Bryce would want something new.

But until then…

Why shouldn't Holden be allowed this?

With an audible breath, he pulled out of Bryce's mouth, hating the feel of the cool air against his spit-soaked shaft.

"You're staying," Holden murmured, not quite a question, but still a repeat from earlier.

Bryce rocked back onto his heels and stared up at Holden. He was utterly debauched, with spit smeared across his chin and tears streaking down his cheeks. His body still shone with sweat, and Holden didn't want to think about the mess Bryce had made on his kitchen floor. But that stopped mattering as soon as Bryce nodded his head yes.

"Let me get you into the bath," he said.

Bryce groaned in protest, but Holden leveled a look at him that cut the sound off before he could finish it.

"If you've taken a vow of silence, I think argumentative noises fall into what's not allowed," he said, helping Bryce to his feet.

"I haven't taken a vow," Bryce countered, words quiet and rough. "But…"

"I know," Holden said quickly, not needing Bryce to finish the thought.

This thing between them was supposed to be sex, a fun exploration of a kink in a safe and controlled environment. Holden hadn't counted on whatever else had come from that space or what it meant for them. It was probably a worry for someone with a clearer head, though, so he ignored it as he plugged the tub and turned on the warm water.

"Is it wrong to say I'd rather sleep covered in sweat if it means your cum will stay in me longer?" Bryce asked, frowning at the tub as it filled.

He looked so despondent in that moment, Holden answered him with the only thing that felt right. He boxed Bryce in against the wall, slanted their mouths together, and he kissed the other man until he was back to speaking in nothing more than sounds. Bryce softly rested his hands against Holden's hips, pressing their chests together and opening his mouth to make more room for Holden's tongue.

Holden's heart did a funny somersault behind his sternum, and he ended the kiss so he could breathe again. He rested his forehead against Bryce's, and the two of them sucked in matching lungfuls of air as Holden came down from whatever high the night had put him on. Bryce was a drug, and Holden needed to be careful or else he'd get addicted.

"It's not wrong," he said.

"You're sure it's okay for me to stay?"

Holden bit the inside of his cheek, nodded his head.

"Will you fuck me again?" Bryce asked.

"Can you handle it?"

"Yes, I...I think so."

Bryce gave him a lopsided smile, and it was all Holden could do to not kiss him again.

"You can stay," he agreed.

"And the fucking?"

Holden chuckled, overwhelmed with a dozen different feelings that had no place existing together at the same time.

"I'll fuck you again," he said. "I'll even keep my dick inside of you after I finish." He skated his fingers down Bryce's ribs, turned him toward the almost full tub. "To keep you full and bursting with it."

Bryce chuckled, accepting Holden's help into the bath.

"You can't say things like that to a man if you don't mean them." Bryce winced as the hot water reached his thighs, but he sank under the surface with a contented little sigh.

Holden's tongue stuck to the roof of his mouth as he watched Bryce get comfortable, watched him float his tattooed fingers on the water.

"I'm going to go change the sheets," he said, because it felt easier than admitting he very much meant the rest of it.

Unfortunately, he also meant all the things he hadn't said.

And that was the worst part of the whole thing.

CHAPTER 10

Bryce

HOLDEN KEPT HIS WORD.

Bryce woke up the next morning with a hard-on between his legs and a soft cock slipping out of his ass. Holden's chest was pressed against his back. The sheets smelled like laundry soap, and the sound of Holden's cell phone alarm was the worst thing Bryce had ever heard.

Holden eased the rest of the way out of him with a grunt, rolling to the nightstand to silence his phone. Bryce turned onto his side and watched Holden flip onto his back, forearm pressed against his eyes. Bryce liked and hated when Holden tried to hide himself. Liked it because it gave him ample opportunity to appreciate the gorgeous physicality of him without being seen, and he hated it because he despised the fact Holden felt it necessary to hide in the first place.

Bryce pressed a kiss against Holden's chest and climbed out of bed. He didn't want to be told to leave, deciding instead to do it on his own terms. His body hurt, though. His legs were so sore from the sex, his balls heavy, and his hole well fucked and tender. He didn't dare reach back to check himself, because he didn't want to make a fool of himself in front of Holden.

After his bath the night before, Holden had fucked him once more, and then they'd fallen asleep with Holden still inside of him. It was the best sleep Bryce had gotten in years. The best night. The best morning. The best lots of things. He stepped into his underwear, hoping he could get back to Merrick's before he made too much a mess of himself, but a quiet groan from the bed stopped him from reaching for his pants. Bryce looked over his shoulder at Holden, now sitting up with his elbows braced against the tops of his thighs.

"It's a little early for regret," Bryce said.

Holden fixed him with a glare. "I think I liked it better when you didn't talk."

"I think I liked it better when you did," he said softly, shoving one leg then the other into his pants.

Holden let out a long breath. "What's your plan, then?"

"I'm going to go back to my brother's place and finish unpacking. Maybe think about finding a job."

"So, you're going to stay in LA?"

Bryce sat down on the edge of the bed, his denim-clad thigh almost pressed against Holden's still naked leg. "That's always been my plan."

"Are you going to stay with Merrick?" Holden asked.

"For now."

Holden rubbed sleep out of one eye with the knuckle of his thumb, bobbing his head in agreement with Bryce's answer. "He can't know about us."

"Is there something to know?" Bryce asked, hating the way his palms had started to sweat. He dried them on the tops of his thighs, then stood up and went in search of his shirt.

"You know what I mean."

"You're right. My brother probably shouldn't know that you come like a fucking faucet."

Holden rolled his eyes. "He probably shouldn't know you guzzle cum like a dying man at an oasis either."

Bryce's cock jerked at the thought of it.

"He shouldn't know the things that come out of your mouth when you're horny," Bryce said next, mouth twitching into a smile. "You're disgusting when you get going."

That earned him a laugh, and Holden stood, looping an arm around Bryce's waist and hauling their bodies back into contact. It felt so good to be close to someone, to be close to Holden.

"He shouldn't know how hard I get for you," Holden whispered into the crook of Bryce's neck. "How I want to tie you to my bed and fuck you until I can't see straight."

"You can't say things like that to a man when you're about to send him home."

Holden's stare danced across Bryce's face, and Bryce's throat went dry at the appraisal. He placed his hands on the slim angles of Holden's hips, waiting….and wanting.

"When can I see you again?" Holden finally asked.

"You're the one who has to go to work."

"You're the one who has to find a job."

Bryce chuckled, pursing his lips. "Finding a job will be easy. I'm a good bartender with a stellar personality. Plus, everyone wants to fuck me."

He'd meant it as a joke, but as soon as the words left his mouth, he regretted them. Something equally dark flashed in Holden's eyes and then the few inches between them felt like miles.

"That's not what I meant," he said quickly.

"But it's true." Holden cleared his throat and took a step back. He didn't have anything on besides his underwear, and Bryce had ruined his opportunity to appreciate the sight of him.

"I don't want to fuck anyone else."

"Okay."

"I didn't go get tested for a one-off," he said, hooking his finger over the waistband of Holden's boxer briefs and dragging the man back toward him. Thankfully, Holden let it happen and Bryce thanked his lucky stars. It was always going to be his mouth that got him in trouble, and he found himself immediately yearning for the night before when the only reason he'd needed to open it was to take Holden's cock into his throat.

"Okay," Holden said again.

"I'm serious."

Holden opened his mouth and Bryce covered it with his hand. "Don't you dare say okay to me one more time. I know I said the wrong thing or I know you took it wrong. That's not how I meant it, and—"

Holden smacked Bryce's hand out of the way, tilting his head to the side sympathetically.

"I know you didn't mean it that way."

"I don't want to fuck anyone else."

"You haven't even been in town for two days," Holden argued. "You don't know that."

Bryce huffed out a laugh, wishing Holden would understand just how much Bryce meant *exactly* that. He'd had plenty of sex over the course of his life, but he'd never—and he meant never—found someone who clicked with him physically in the ways Holden had. Never mind the immediate attraction between them, their chemistry in bed was undeniable. Bryce wasn't about to go out looking to replicate it...or jeopardize it.

"I don't want to fuck anyone else," he repeated, sliding his hand into Holden's underwear and squeezing his dick. "I've dreamed about this cock my whole life, you know."

Holden's eyes sparkled with amusement, and the air in the room lightened.

Perfect, Bryce hadn't ruined everything yet.

"Your whole life?"

Bryce nodded, giving Holden's shaft a stroke.

"Dreamed about your mouth and your hands too," he

murmured, leaning in close and brushing his mouth against Holden's parted lips.

"So you're saying I'm the man of your dreams?"

He laughed and kissed Holden then, feeling brave.

Instead of taking charge as he had the night before, Holden let himself be kissed. He went pliant under Bryce's touch, groaning when Bryce took him back down to the bed, spread himself out over the top of Holden's mostly naked body. Bryce was still hard, but Holden was nowhere near it. That didn't stop Bryce from grinding against him, from rubbing their bodies together.

"You might be," he said on an exhale.

Holden grabbed him by the hips and flipped him onto his back. He notched his knee up beneath Bryce's balls and pressed until Bryce's eyes rolled back and he went quiet.

"You could be the man of mine," Holden teased. "If you would stop talking so much."

A box of butterflies opened in Bryce's stomach, and he pretended to zip his lips and toss away the key. He couldn't read the expression on Holden's face, and he worried again he'd said the wrong thing or gone too far. But Holden leaned down and kissed him again, hard and insistent. There was no tongue in it, no spit, just rough desperation, and then a cold gust of air as Holden climbed off the top of him.

Bryce pushed himself into a seated position, watching Holden fidget with his hands. He stood and adjusted himself. Leaving Holden's bed was proving to be much harder than he'd expected. Bryce forced himself to finish getting dressed, keeping his eyes on the floor because it was apparently impossible for him to look at Holden and not lose his fucking mind.

"When do you want to see me again?" he asked after getting his shoes on. He had his phone, three ignored texts from Merrick, his wallet, and his keys.

"No one has ever asked it that way."

Holden had moved to the couch, still far too undressed for Bryce's sanity.

"Well." Bryce shrugged helplessly.

"I want to see you after you get a job," Holden said.

Of all the answers Bryce had expected, that hadn't been one of them.

"Who knows when that will be."

"You said it would be easy." Holden smirked at him. "Consider it incentive."

"You're mean."

"I could be," he agreed. "If you'd like that."

Bryce shivered, breaking eye contact to stare at the ceiling. "I won't be able to get a job if I walk into every place with a hard-on. It'll scare the clientele."

"I figured the hard-on was part of the 'everyone wanting to fuck you' thing."

Bryce's jaw fell open and he stared at Holden, feeling more like a gaping fish than a man. "Did you just make that into a joke?"

Holden shrugged one shoulder toward his ear.

"Fine," Bryce said, an unnerving lightness blooming in his chest. "I'll go get a job."

"Good."

"How will we celebrate?"

"I haven't decided," Holden said simply.

"Do I get a say in the festivities?"

"As much of a say as you had last night."

Bryce's eyelashes fluttered in a very embarrassing way. "Okay," he rasped.

"Is it?"

"Very."

Holden's tongue traced across the plump curve of his lower lip and his stare roamed over Bryce's burning hot cheeks.

"Are you sure?"

Bryce managed an abbreviated nod, turning his entire body away from Holden. He bracketed his hands on his hips, sucking in an embarrassingly loud breath of air.

"You can't keep doing this to a man," he complained.

Holden let out a soft laugh. "What am I doing?"

"Reducing me to nothing more than bones and muscles and *want*."

"I can stop," Holden suggested.

Bryce dipped his chin toward his chest in defeat. "Please don't."

"Get out of here, Bryce," Holden said gently. "Go let your brother know you're alive, go find a job, do the things you need to do, alright? I'll be here when you're done."

He wanted to turn around and kiss Holden, but knew if he saw Holden there on the couch with all that skin and those blue eyes and that amazing mouth, he'd get drawn right back into bed. He had things to do, Holden had to go to work, and he'd never meant for this to happen. Everything he wanted to say tangled in his throat, so he nodded, then let himself out of Holden's apartment. He didn't look back, but maybe that was for the best.

CHAPTER 11

Holden

AFTER BRYCE LEFT, Holden went to work. He tried to ignore Merrick, as usual, but his co-worker made it nearly impossible. No wonder Bryce was so happy being forced into silence. It had to be a better option than trying to keep up with Merrick's never-ending stream of chatter.

"My brother is out looking for a job today," Merrick said at some point, which unfortunately caught Holden's attention. He glanced up from the rose he was tattooing on the inside of someone's wrist, but offered no verbal encouragement for Merrick to continue. Of course, he did anyway. "I think it means he wants to stay."

"Was that not the point?"

"I hoped he'd want to stay, but I can never assume."

Holden hummed and wiped the excess ink off his client's arm.

"I think he's already met someone," Merrick went on, and Holden stared hard at the lines of the rose tattoo before dipping into some ink to finish the shading on the smallest petal.

"He didn't come home last night."

"Good for him."

Merrick made a dismissive sound. "It's not a shock. Bryce has always been…"

"A ladies' man?" Holden supplied.

"A slut," Merrick finished.

Holden rolled his stool back and frowned at Merrick. He wanted to call out the comment, but he couldn't without drawing attention to himself…or to Bryce.

"I think he uses his body as a way to get attention," Merrick went on, but Holden had already had enough.

"I don't think this is appropriate conversation for work," he said.

Merrick laughed, unbothered. "This is a shop."

"Well, have the conversation with yourself then."

He'd already said too much, and he felt the weight of Merrick's stare on him as he set to finishing the walk-in tattoo. It didn't take much more than five minutes to get through the last of the shading and the highlighting. He cleaned all the blood and ink residue before wrapping his client's wrist with plastic wrap and medical tape. Merrick grumbled under his breath about Saniderm again, and Holden ignored him entirely.

After getting his client set up with aftercare instructions and taking their cash—always appreciated—he went to clean up his station, keeping his back to Merrick for as much of the process as he could manage.

Ink and Ember was a small shop, and he and Merrick were the first artists hired to work for the owner, Riggs. There was room for one other artist, but Riggs had been holding off on filling the rental, probably because he hadn't even wanted to hire Merrick and Holden in the first place. Holden was grateful for the opportunity. The shop was close to home and Riggs was a fair boss. The only downfall of the place was Merrick and his mouth, but Merrick had brought Holden Bryce so it couldn't really be all that bad.

He hated that he thought of Bryce as a good addition to

his life. He didn't even know the other man. They'd spent more time fucking than they'd spent talking, and maybe that had been by design. Bryce could keep up with Merrick but didn't want to. Holden didn't make him, so there was appeal for Bryce when he looked at him. Even if what Merrick said was true, even if Bryce had a promiscuous past, none of that mattered to Holden. He'd gotten tested, they were safe together, and they were having fun.

It was more than fun, though. Holden knew that already.

He liked the way Bryce looked with a mouthful of cock, and he liked waking up with his dick still in Bryce's ass. Those were the kinds of things he could get used to, even if he didn't trust them to stay. Whatever he had going on with Bryce could be a for-now thing, and that would be fine.

Even if his heart argued with him about it.

Thankfully, the rose was his last tattoo of the day and he didn't need to sit through any more forced conversation with Merrick about his brother. Holden finished cleaning his station and checked his phone for a message from Bryce. There wasn't one, which was somehow surprising and not. He wondered if Bryce was as spooked by their time together as he was.

Holden needed to clear his head, to make sure he wasn't reading too much into nothing. He had a tendency to do that, at least he did when he was younger. Holden had always gone all in on things, love and art included. So after saying goodbye to Merrick and Riggs, he locked himself in his car and called the one person he knew could talk sense into him.

"Baby brother," his sister greeted, flashing him a smile as her face filled his screen.

Hannah was the spitting image of their mother with her long dark hair and equally bright blue eyes. They were features Holden shared, even if he preferred to bleach his hair or color it differently. Hannah had their mother's smile and nose where Holden's facial features were more aligned with their father, but there was no missing the family resemblance when any of them were together.

"Hey, Hannah."

"You look distressed." The image of his sister jostled as she set her phone down and made work of preparing to talk to him in the way she always did when she thought he needed help. "Are things not working out at the shop?"

"The shop is fine," he promised.

"Even with the talker?"

Holden pushed his hair out of his face and dropped his head against the headrest with a groan. "Merrick is Merrick," he said simply. "Did you know he has a brother?"

"I didn't know that because you never told me."

"He has a brother."

"In LA?" she asked.

He nodded. "He just got here a couple days ago from St. Jack's Bay."

Hannah's eyebrow lifted slightly.

"His name is Bryce," Holden went on, and his sister's smile brightened.

"I bet it is. Tell me more."

"There's not much more to say."

"You like him," she stated.

"I don't know him."

"But what you do know."

Holden bit the inside of his cheek and glared at his sister. She knew him too well, but that was what he wanted. That was why he'd called her. He needed someone to talk him off the ledge about Bryce and who better to do that than his meddling, therapist sister.

"I like how I feel when he's around," Holden admitted.

"So he doesn't talk as much as Merrick?"

He shook his head, then nodded. "The two of them together are a lot, but when it's just him…"

Holden trailed off, flashing back to the grateful tears that slicked from the corners of Bryce's eyes when he had no choice except to shut up. The peaceful quiet between them, punctuated only by the sound of skin against skin and Bryce's desperate breaths.

"Oh, you love him," Hannah said, which was enough to snap Holden out of his memories.

"No."

"I know that look," she said.

"I don't know him."

"You've never needed to." Hannah tilted her head to the side, eyes sparkling. "You've always fallen in love with ideas first."

"It's never gotten me anywhere good."

"It's gotten you here," she reminded him. "To this point. To these moments."

"Yeah," he reluctantly conceded.

"What does Donovan think?"

Holden scoffed. "I've barely talked to him since he moved to San Diego. He's been busy with whatever he has going on down there."

"Do you not have anyone else you can talk to?"

The implication was clear, even if she didn't mean any harm by it. Holden had a habit of putting all his eggs in one basket. All his energy into one friend or one partner and when those relationships fell away, he found himself alone again. It was another reason he'd grown so used to the quiet in his life. He regarded it more as a companion than a threat.

"Making friends as an adult is stupid," he told her.

Hannah laughed. "Yeah, but you should try it sometime."

As soon as the words left her mouth, a text from Bryce flashed across his screen. His sister must have seen the excitement on his face, because she leaned back and laughed at him as he swiped to read it.

BRYCE

Might have found a job.

Have you ever heard of a club called
Rapture?

No, but that's good.

I just finished talking to the owners. Do you
want to come meet me for a drink? If you're
off work.

He'd finished work and his only plans had involved going home and trying to pretend he wasn't waiting to hear from Bryce.

Me: Sure. Send me the address.

"Do you need to go?" Hannah asked him.

"He wants me to meet him for a drink at a bar he might be getting a job at."

"That's sweet." Her smile fell away and her expression turned serious. "There's nothing wrong with the way you love people, Holden."

"I know," he agreed, even if he didn't believe it entirely.

"Say it."

"There's nothing wrong with the way I love people."

"Will you call me tomorrow? Let me know how it goes?" she asked.

"I'll text."

"I'll take it." Her smile was back and she picked up her phone. "I love you. And I'm lucky to be loved *by* you."

"Love you too, Hannah."

He hung up the phone before she could, the screen flashing with a text from Bryce that had a dropped pin location for him to follow. The bar wasn't in Silverlake or anywhere near it, which was not ideal, but getting to Pasadena so late at night shouldn't be too hard. He hoped the place wasn't fancy because he was dressed for work in sneakers and jeans and a t-shirt that probably had ink stains on it somewhere.

Holden made it to Pasadena and double-checked the location Bryce had sent him because he'd ended up in a dirt parking lot behind a massive church. He sent Bryce a text to confirm.

> Not sure I'm in the right place

Bryce answered quickly, like he'd been holding his phone.

> lol you are. I'll meet you outside.

Holden turned off his car and headed for the steps, his breath hitching a little when the massive wooden doors swung open and Bryce's silhouette appeared.

"Pretty cool, huh?" Bryce asked, stretching his hand out for Holden.

He was too caught off-guard to do anything besides slide his palm against Bryce's and let the other man haul him up the rest of the stairs.

"I found this place entirely on accident," Bryce started yammering immediately, and Holden had to admit he found it briefly endearing. "I was looking for something else and it turns out they were looking for a new bartender, and I thought two birds, one stone, right?

"What were you looking for?"

In lieu of an answer, Holden let Bryce pull him into the entry of the church, which had been repurposed as a coat check and security desk. He had to give his ID and sign a release form, which felt very serious for a bar, but Bryce still hadn't answered the question.

Once they were through the second set of doors, Holden tripped over his own feet. They were definitely in a church, or what used to be a church. At some point, it had been converted into a club and bar. There was a staircase that hugged the front wall and what looked like the old choir loft upstairs.

"What kind of club is this?" he asked.

Bryce dragged him to the bar against the back wall.

"Callum, this is Holden. Holden, this is Callum. He's one of the bartenders here."

"Nice to meet you," Holden said automatically.

Callum had a nice-looking face, kind eyes, and a band around his left ring finger. "Maybe we'll be seeing more of you if Bryce gets hired."

"Probably," Bryce agreed, and Holden swallowed hard.

Maybe he wasn't the only person who'd accidentally gone all in on his feelings with a complete stranger.

"Do you want a beer?" Bryce asked.

He managed a nod and Callum served them both a basic lager in a brown bottle and left them alone. It was early and the club was fairly empty, but judging by the space, the weekends were probably pretty busy.

"How was your interview?" Holden asked.

"I think it went well."

"Callum seems to think so."

"Yeah." Bryce scooted closer. "His husband is real good friends with the owner."

Holden took a drink and turned to survey the club, the glint of movement in the loft catching his eye, a flash of bare skin.

"What kind of club is this?" he asked for hopefully the third and final time.

Bryce exhaled a soft laugh and turned in the same direction as Holden, angled his face up toward the second floor and answered, "It's a kink club."

CHAPTER 12

Bryce

BRYCE HAD WATCHED a lot of porn in his life, so when he walked into Rapture to meet the owner and main bartender, the furniture hadn't been unsettling. Seeing real life people spanking each other was different from seeing it on his phone, though, and he had to admit, he liked it better. Not that there was anything wrong with porn. Bryce loved porn, but the shock value of production made some of the scenes feel a little over the top. What he observed while he waited for Landon and Callum felt exceedingly intimate to watch, almost like he wasn't supposed to be there.

The interview went well, and he realized his being asked to come during operational hours was a deliberate choice by the owner. It made sense because if you couldn't get through a conversation without gawking at what was happening in the background, you'd never be able to make it through a shift. Bryce wanted to make it through a shift.

Landon said they'd be in touch, and then Bryce asked if he could stay and have a couple of drinks. Landon explained there was a no drinking on the clock rule, but other than that, since he wasn't hired yet, he was welcome. There was also a no fraternization rule, but Callum told Bryce that one was much less strict than the no drinking rule. Bryce didn't care so much about that because the only person he wanted to fraternize with was Holden.

"A kink club," Holden repeated, rubbing the bridge of his nose.

"Pretty cool, right?" he repeated.

"And you want to work here?"

"I want to work," he said.

Holden nodded and took a drink.

"Does it bother you?"

"Does it matter?"

Bryce shrugged. It shouldn't matter, but it kind of did. He also didn't want to admit that out loud and he sort of wished he'd never asked the question.

"I don't care where you work," Holden finally said. "I don't mean like I don't *care*. I just…don't care."

Bryce let out a quick laugh and knocked their shoulders together. "So you don't care."

Holden glared at him, then turned his attention back to the dance floor.

"Did you even know this place was here?" Bryce asked.

"No."

"Did you think it was a church?"

"I don't come to Pasadena often," Holden explained. "It's a bit of a drive."

"Oh. Right." Bryce took another swallow of his drink and groaned. "Well, thank you for coming. For me, I mean. To have a drink."

"Normally I have to gag you to get you to stop talking," Holden said quietly, barely loud enough to hear over the music. "Why are you all tangled up in yourself now?"

Bryce didn't have an answer that was a good one. Well, he had the truth, but the truth was embarrassing. He was having a hard time talking to Holden because Holden had worked the whole day, then driven up to Pasadena to have a drink with him, and he didn't complain about the traffic or anything. And the two of them were standing in the middle of a kink club having a drink together and that felt a lot like a date, which was nothing they'd done before. Nothing they'd even discussed. But he couldn't say all of that to Holden without sounding like a crazy person, so instead he asked the second-best thing.

"Is this a date?"

Holden's jaw went slack, and Bryce wanted to bury himself in a hole. Bryce tried to not look as mortified as he felt while Holden finished his drink, set the empty bottle down on the bar, and faced Bryce head on.

"Do you want it to be?" he asked.

"God. That's not what you signed up for, is it? You took me for a sandwich, and it really just escalated from there, didn't it? It wasn't supposed to be anything serious, and now here I am—"

"You got tested so I could fuck you raw." Holden grabbed his face, fingers pressed into one side and thumb into the other, puckering Bryce's mouth like a fish. "That feels serious."

Bryce was glad he couldn't speak. That again, Holden had made it impossible.

"Do you want it to be?" Holden asked again.

Bryce nodded.

"Is there some place we can go sit down?"

Holden released his mouth, and Bryce hated it. He worked his jaw to loosen it, then motioned toward a wrought iron staircase against the back wall. "There's a loft. It's a little quieter, but a lot raunchier."

Holden's stare flickered toward the loft and he gestured dismissively. "Lead the way."

Bryce's heart was in his throat, but he led Holden to the back of the club and up the stairs. There was a leather couch against one wall, a small bar, and a St. Andrew's cross in the corner. There were private rooms in the hall; Landon had told him as much during the interview, but all those doors were closed. Bryce didn't know if they were occupied or not, but before he could look, Holden sat down on the couch and patted the empty cushion to his right. Bryce sat beside him, fingers nervously picking at the label of his beer.

"I don't want you to talk unless you're talking about yourself," Holden said. "In a meaningful way. I don't want you to fill the silence."

Bryce hated that, but he liked Holden more.

He took a drink of his beer and settled into the couch, tucked halfway against Holden's side. The other man made himself comfortable, and Bryce was jealous of the way silence came so easy for Holden. Bryce had never imagined a life like that, one where he could just exist without needing to fight for it. But he *could* imagine it, if he was being honest with himself. He'd already had a taste of it, a sweet gift from a man who didn't really know him from his brother but also didn't care.

"I've felt more myself since I got to LA than I have in the past three years," he said.

Holden raised a brow. "Why?"

"It feels like a fresh start a little."

"Why did you leave home?"

"It was time for a change of scenery," he said. "Also I wanted to get away from an ex."

"Abuse?" Holden asked.

Bryce took a swig of his beer and set the bottle down on a low table in front of them. "No, just...we weren't compatible."

"How long were you together for?"

"Too long," he answered. "Almost three years."

Bryce watched as the gears clicked into place about his earlier comment. Holden licked his lips, brow knit together like he wanted to say something but thought better of it.

"I know you don't like to talk," Bryce said quickly, "but I wish you'd say whatever just crossed your mind."

"It was something your brother said."

Bryce groaned, scrubbing a hand down his face and dropping his head against the back of the couch. The leather was already warm against his skin.

"He thinks I'm promiscuous."

"That wasn't the word." The corner of Holden's mouth twitched. "But yes."

"I went a little wild after the breakup. Maybe not the best way to nurse my wounds."

"Also not for him to judge. And not me either."

It was in his nature to defend himself, to try and justify the choices he'd made after breaking up with Bella, but Bryce knew that wasn't what Holden wanted from him in that moment. The instruction had been clear—no speaking unless it was meaningful and his defense was not that. Not because it didn't matter, but because it didn't matter to Holden. This was the fresh start Bryce had hoped for by coming to LA, and the fresh start he had found.

"Merrick has opinions," he finally said.

Holden frowned. "I don't want to talk about your brother."

"We'll have to eventually. If this is a date. Or rather, if we're planning to have more dates than this one." Bryce paused and licked his lips. "Did you want to have more than this one?"

"I didn't even know we were having this one until I got here," Holden said, a chunk of hair falling over his eye. "But I'm not against more."

"Are we just going to keep it from him?"

"It's not his business who you date and it's certainly not his business who I date."

Bryce chuckled under his breath. "He told me before I came that I'd think you were cute."

Holden's brows shot toward his hairline. "Is that so?"

"Well, he thinks I'll think everyone is cute probably." Bryce tried to shrug off the confession.

"Do you?"

"No."

Holden made a thoughtful sound in the back of his throat and turned his stare squarely onto Bryce.

"Do you want to stay here longer or do you want to go?"

"Complicated," Holden answered.

"Try me."

"I want you to suck my dick," Holden admitted. "But I don't want to jeopardize your chances of getting hired. I also want to stay here because I'm comfortable and I want you to keep talking. I'm afraid if I take you home, we'll end up in bed."

"Bed is not a bad place to be, but hold on. You *want* me to keep talking?" Bryce laughed, slid off the couch, and landed on his knees between Holden's spread legs. "I don't think you can have both of those things at the same time."

Bryce smoothed his hands up the tops of Holden's thighs, eyes going heavy with want. Holden swallowed hard and undid the button on his jeans and pulled down the fly. His cock was already almost hard, pressing against the material of his underwear and fighting against the undone zipper.

"How about I suck your dick first, then we have another drink. I can talk some more, and then we can go back to your house and end up in bed?"

Holden pulled his dick out from behind the waistband of his boxer briefs and smeared the tip across Bryce's mouth.

"That sounds like a nice..."

Bryce kept his eyes open and closed his lips around the middle of Holden's shaft, taking as much of his length as he could manage without throwing up all over himself. Holden groaned, fisting Bryce's hair, hips lifting off the couch to chase the heat of Bryce's throat. Bryce kept his stare locked on

Holden's face, committing every flicker and sigh of pleasure to memory.

Merrick had been wrong about Bryce, about the things he'd done after the breakup with Bella. Yeah, there was a little bit of sluttiness Bryce wanted to get out of his system after being monogamous for so many years with someone who didn't please him sexually, but that hadn't been the real reason. Or at least, the reason he kept it up as long as he had.

For Bryce, sex gave him a chance to be present in his body.

There was no need to drown out Merrick's voice or fight for his voice to be heard. Sex was a time where there didn't need to be words, but he was still able to communicate. And he had that again, now, with Holden, even though it was different than it had been before. With everyone else, the sex had been quiet and as soon as it was over, Bryce found himself right back in the noise.

Holden kept him quiet, kept him soft.

Holden himself was the opposite of soft, his cock growing thicker and longer against the roof of Bryce's mouth with every thrust.

"Look at me," Holden rasped, tugging Bryce's hair until he fought his eyes back open. Bryce wanted to watch, he wanted to look, but it was so easy to get lost in Holden, in the prize he offered with his body and his time.

Holden took Bryce's head into his hands, one on either side, and he started to thrust. Slow at first, shallow pumps of his hips that pushed his cock into Bryce's mouth. But as the pleasure grew between them, Holden's movements turned more frantic, less smooth. His thumbs around the edge of Bryce's eyes, angling his face the way he wanted, and then without any warning at all, Holden came.

Hot jets of cum shot against the back of Bryce's tongue, one landing in his throat and making him choke. Holden held him still, riding out the rest of his pleasure on Bryce's tongue and against the roof of his mouth. After his balls emptied,

Holden went limp against the couch, fingers still tangled in Bryce's hair. They both caught their breath, and Bryce's lashes fluttered closed.

Holden was perfect for him and he hated it.

Really.

CHAPTER 13

Holden

HOLDEN HAD NEVER BEEN in love, but the way Bryce
hooked their fingers together and allowed himself to be led
out of the club had Holden wondering if this might be what it
felt like. His body buzzed with anticipation as he walked
Bryce into the parking lot, straight to Merrick's car.

"Have you been bringing your brother's car over for our
hookups?" Holden asked.

Bryce unlocked the door and sank down into the driver's
seat.

"Sometimes. Sometimes I use an Uber."

Holden chuckled and leaned down, one hand braced
against the top of the car, the other on the driver's door. "Are
you coming over?"

"I don't know." Bryce's answer was breathy. "Am I?"

"I think so."

Bryce nodded and Holden stepped out of the way so he
could close the door. There were no parting words, no affec-
tion. Holden's feelings were far too close to the surface to risk
letting any of them out. He was falling for Bryce and that
hadn't ever been part of the plan. They'd talked about it a

little, the last night at his house, but had that meant anything official?

God, he was pathetic.

On the way back to his apartment, he picked apart every conversation he'd had with Bryce, trying to make sense of what they were to each other. When he parked, Bryce was already there. They walked to his front door together, fingers barely brushing for how close they were. Bryce crowded him in when he tried to unlock the door and much to his embarrassment, he fumbled the keys. It took an eternity, but they finally made it inside, and when Holden locked the door, all the air left the room.

"You look distraught," Bryce said slowly, toeing off his shoes and kicking them into the corner near the front door. "Is everything all right?"

"I'm just thinking too hard."

"About?"

"You. Obviously." Holden slid his hands around Bryce's waist and walked them both into the living room until Bryce's thighs hit the arm of the couch.

"If you keep talking like that, it'll go to my head."

"You're the one who told me I had the cock of your dreams. How do you think that made me feel?" Holden teased, tracing his fingers over the waistband of Bryce's jeans.

"Hopefully like you were the best lay in the world."

Holden chuckled and nodded. "I mean, yeah."

"I'm sensing a but." Bryce leaned in and nipped Holden's lower lip.

He could take the conversation two ways. Holden could admit he was developing actual feelings for Bryce and see what happened, or he could shrug it off and give Bryce a reason to stop talking. The latter would have been the most appealing one a handful of days ago, but that didn't seem to be the case anymore. Holden felt greedy and he wanted both, but he didn't want to put himself—and his heart—on the line.

"No buts," he lied.

Bryce pulled back, dark eyes searching Holden's face for the real answer. Bryce must not have found it because he frowned and hoisted himself onto the arm of the couch, then over it entirely. He collapsed onto his back with a loud exhale and scooted into the corner, away from Holden. It wasn't a deflective move, but the intent was to put space between them and it had worked. Holden was frozen with the fronts of his legs against the side of the couch, his cock traitorously hard against his thigh.

"Permission to speak freely," Bryce murmured.

"Alright."

Bryce popped the button of his jeans undone and tugged down the zipper, then slid his hand into his underwear and grabbed his cock. He arched his back and moaned, throat bobbing as he swallowed, and it was impossible for Holden to not imagine the way Bryce's throat thickened when Holden shoved his dick into it.

"I don't want to fuck anyone else," Bryce said. "I know you don't believe that, but it's true. Even if I met someone else who I found attractive..." His hand moved slowly, stroking from root to tip, and Holden's stare darted from Bryce's wrist to his face and back again.

"Even if?" he prompted.

Bryce laughed under his breath. "Look at you. *Wanting* me to talk for once."

He didn't just want it.

He needed it.

A sudden and unexpected fear took root at the base of his spine, the knowledge everything was on the precipice of changing. Only he couldn't tell if the change was for better or worse.

"I haven't even looked at anyone else since I met you," Bryce went on, talking as leisurely as he touched himself. "All I think about is you."

"All I think about is you," Holden said back.

Bryce's mouth twitched into a smile, and he adjusted his pants to reveal the slick and swollen tip of his cock. He kept stroking himself, eyes locked on Holden, who hadn't moved except to breathe.

"Is it childish to want to call you my boyfriend?"

Holden swallowed hard. "I don't think so."

"You like how it sounds?"

Holden nodded, and Bryce flipped onto his hands and knees, crawling back to the side of the couch where Holden stood. They were both still completely dressed, and Bryce jerked his chin.

"Let me see you," he whispered. "Let me look at my boyfriend."

Holden reached back and grabbed the loose material of his shirt to tug it over his head. He tossed it onto the floor and then pushed his jeans down to his ankles, stepping out of the tight denim. His underwear went next, then his socks, and Bryce watched him the whole time like he was a dessert buffet being unveiled.

"I want to see you too," Holden finally managed to say.

Bryce wiggled out of his clothes, and his bare skin made the arch of his back look even more indecent.

"Don't move," Holden murmured and Bryce smiled wide at him in reply.

Holden grabbed a bottle of lube and then manhandled Bryce so his chest pressed against the back of the couch and his legs spread wide enough to make room for Holden behind him. He tossed the lube onto a cushion and spread Bryce's ass apart and buried his face into the sweaty heat. Bryce bucked and cried out, and Holden pushed him down against the couch so his meal wasn't interrupted. He sucked and kissed Bryce's hole, groaning at the taste of him.

"Jesus Christ, I'm so fucking lucky my boyfriend knows how to eat ass."

Holden slapped his hand against the side of Bryce's thigh in warning. "Shut up."

"God, there he is."

Holden dug his fingers into Bryce's skin and got back to work. He made a sloppy mess of Bryce's ass, then made quick work of slicking his cock and leveraging himself up onto the couch. He pushed his shaft into Bryce's spit-soaked hole and bit the inside of his cheek to stop himself from coming on the spot.

Bryce muttered a curse, reaching back and grabbing Holden's thigh to support himself on the edge of the couch. Holden breathed hard, burying his face into the crook of Bryce's neck to catch his breath.

"Please kiss me," Bryce said next, and Holden screwed his eyes closed. "I want to taste myself on you."

There was no way Holden could tell him no, so he gave Bryce what he wanted. What they both wanted. He slanted their mouths together and pushed his tongue past Bryce's teeth, and then he started to move. The positioning was far from perfect, but the need to get deep was primal. Holden rutted up, slamming their bodies together while trying to keep their mouths fused. Bryce reached around and started to stroke his dick, his entire body tensing and grabbing onto Holden for dear life.

They'd had sex before, but nothing like this. This was awkward and frantic, and it was fucking beyond hot.

There was no role play happening between them, no gags and no rules, just an urgency Holden had never experienced with another partner. Sweat prickled the back of his neck, and Bryce didn't stop talking. He wasn't making much sense, but even when Holden kissed him, Bryce's mouth never stopped. And much to his surprise, Holden found it didn't bother him. With their bodies fused together, slick and wanting, Bryce spoke freely. It was different from a normal conversation, less insistent but just as important.

"Hush," Holden finally whispered, bracketing an arm around the front of Bryce's chest and pinning their bodies together. He slowed his pace until Bryce closed his mouth, and then he shoved Bryce down into the cushions and really started to fuck him. Bryce's words turned to moans, turned to whimpers, turned to cries. It was unrestrained and it was perfect.

"Where do you want me to come?" Holden asked, already on the edge of an orgasm he knew would make him see stars.

"Everywhere," Bryce begged. "Deep."

Holden slammed himself home, slamming his cock so deep into Bryce the tip of it kissed the soft second hole. Bryce screamed and trembled, and Holden came. He grabbed Bryce's hips so hard he was sure to leave bruises, but he needed to ground himself or risk losing his heart entirely. He came with his whole body, his heartbeat pounding in his ears, his pulse heavy and insistent in the center of his shaft. Holden spilled deep into Bryce's body, and Bryce came all over his hand, all over Holden's couch. Holden's orgasm went on forever, and he folded himself over Bryce's back, kissed the sweaty dip between his shoulder blades.

Beneath him, Bryce's entire body shivered, and Holden managed to move them both onto the floor so neither of them had to hold themselves up. His cock still pulsed even though there was nothing left to spill, and he rested his forehead against the back of Bryce's neck.

"Do you have a plug?" Bryce managed to ask, reaching back and digging his nails into Holden's thigh.

"What?"

"Do you have a plug you can put in me? To keep your cum there."

Holden's dick managed to find some more cum, another dribble of it leaking out of his slit.

"I have a plug."

"Please." Bryce's voice cracked, an unignorable kind of

desperation in his tone that had Holden pulling out of the other man and clambering to the other side of the studio to get a plug out of the nightstand.

When he came back, Bryce had moved onto all fours, back bowed with his ass up, cheek pressed against the hardwood floor.

"I didn't want it to come out," he murmured.

Holden's breath caught in his throat, and he carefully petted his hands down Bryce's spine before easing the plug into his still wet and stretched hole. The silicone toy popped into Bryce's body and, in response, Bryce let out a gasping breath that sounded a lot like a sob.

"Hey." Holden traced his fingers up Bryce's ribs and shoulder and neck until he reached Bryce's face. "You're okay."

Bryce didn't say anything, but he let Holden pull him into his lap, one leg on either side. He took Bryce's face into his hands, making note of his tear-stained cheeks and his chapped lips. He brought Bryce's face down to his and pressed their mouths together, swallowing down another strangled cry.

He wasn't the only one fighting back some insecurities, it seemed. One thing he knew for certain was he had no intention of making Bryce face his alone. Holden stroked his thumbs across Bryce's cheeks and kissed the salt tracks from the corner of his mouth.

Holden was so obviously falling in love with this man. Bryce, who was his opposite in every way but also Bryce who somehow fit into all the nooks and crannies he'd never realized needed filling. Because Holden loved his quiet and he loved his peace, but he loved Bryce just as much. Maybe someday he would love Bryce more.

"Hey," Holden whispered again, ready to find out. "Bryce. Bryce. Talk to me."

CHAPTER 14

Bryce

THE ABSOLUTE LAST thing Bryce wanted to do was talk. His asshole was filled with cum, a plug kept him stretched, and Holden's mouth moved across his face with a dangerously slow pace that would have had Bryce's knees weak if he had to stand up.

"I'm fine," he muttered. "Just overwhelmed."

"Do you need me to take the plug out? Do you need some water? What do you need?"

Holden was adorable when he was panicked, and it was all Bryce could do to not laugh about it. Not in a mean way. In an *I'm very much already in love with you* kind of way.

"No, all of that is perfect. You're perfect."

The confession seemed to settle Holden a little. He leaned against the back of the couch, hands resting on the swell of Bryce's hips.

"Talk to me," Holden said softly.

Bryce snickered at that, raising a brow. "Are you sure that's what you want?"

"Not normally," Holden teased. "But yes, now."

"I just went from having nothing back home to having

everything here. I mean, I don't have my own apartment and I don't have a car, but—"

"Or a job."

Bryce knocked his elbow into Holden's arm, and the other man smiled at him with so much warmth, Bryce almost melted.

"I actually do have a job," he said, smugly. "Landon from Rapture called when I was on my way over here to offer it to me."

Holden smiled at him again, crashing a chaste and excited kiss against his lips.

"Congratulations."

"Mmmn, yes, more of that. But point being, well on the way to the rest of it. And there's you. There...I have you."

It felt like a risky thing to say out loud, even though they'd *just* had the boyfriend conversation. Bryce didn't entirely feel like he could trust it, but he wanted to. Oh, fuck, how he wanted to.

"You have me," Holden agreed, dropping another kiss against his mouth. "Can I have you again?"

"I don't know how you have another orgasm in you."

"Who said anything about orgasms?" Holden reached back and pressed up on the flared base of the plug, pushing it deeper into Bryce's body. "Being bare inside of you is just as good as coming in you."

Bryce's shoulders trembled on an exhale. "I want that so much, but I have my brother's car and I have to get home."

Holden's mouth made a dry clicking sound, but he nodded his understanding. "We should get you cleaned up and ready to go back to his place, then."

"I don't want to go."

"I don't want you to go but you can sleep over soon. I'll take you all night long if that's what you want."

Bryce shivered. "You'll gag me again?"

"If you like."

"I do," he murmured.

"This is going to sound really weird, but would you like it if I bought fake cum?" Holden's cheeks darkened with the question, and Bryce parted his lips to speak but his tongue stuck to the roof of his mouth and no sound came out.

"Is that too much?" Holden scrunched his nose, covering his face with both hands. "I know you said you weren't into the pregnancy part of it, but I just thought—"

"I've never," he interrupted, pulling Holden's hands away from his face. "I've never thought about it. No one has brought it up."

Holden bit his bottom lip.

Bryce tugged it free. "Tell me more."

Holden was back as he'd been the first day they met, silent and reserved. But even without using words, his face telegraphed everything he was feeling, all of the want and curiosity that had existed between them from the very first meeting.

"Tell me more, or I won't stop talking," he tried, drawing in a breath and hoping Holden gave him an answer because Bryce had no idea what to say. He loved that Holden was willing to gag him and he loved being gagged, but he'd never felt pressured to speak when it was just the two of them together. It wasn't anything like his life back home.

"God, you're a menace." Holden groaned, pushing harder on the plug which definitely drew a noise out of Bryce, but nothing coherent. "I know you like the idea of being filled, the act of it. They sell like, I don't know, fake cum. We could fuck and I would still come in you, but I could use some of that so you could leak…if you wanted."

Bryce rubbed his lower lip, a sudden itch that refused to go away. That was possibly the most Holden had ever said to him, but also the sweetest thing anyone had ever offered him in his entire adult life.

"Would you like it?" he asked.

"I don't know. But I'll try it."

"That might be the most romantic thing anyone has ever done for me." A fresh wave of tears threatened the corners of his eyes, but Bryce was absolutely not going to cry over his boyfriend offering to pump him full of fake jizz.

"That can't be true," Holden said with a laugh. "But we'll see. Until then, I think you were trying to say you needed to get back to your brother's place."

"I take it back."

Holden laughed and smacked the outside of his thigh. "Let's get you cleaned up."

With as much reluctance as his tired body could manage, Bryce protested the attention for five seconds before quickly giving in and letting Holden walk him into the shower. He didn't even pretend to hate it when Holden washed his body and his hair, and he had no fight in him at all when Holden toweled him off.

"Can I ask for something?"

"You can ask for everything," Bryce murmured as Holden helped him back into his clothes.

"Before you go to sleep tonight, when you take the plug out, will you record it and send it to me?"

Another flare of heat burned behind Bryce's sternum, and he managed to nod his agreement.

"I know you like the cum inside of you, but would you push some out while you're filming? Then if you want to, you can scoop it back inside."

Bryce had obviously died and gone to heaven. "You make it hard to want to leave."

Holden finished buttoning Bryce's jeans, then slanted their mouths together and kissed him until both of them were near the front door again, breathing frantic.

"I don't work Sunday," Holden whispered. "Spend the night Saturday?"

"Absolutely."

"Drive safe," he said next.

"I'll do my best."

Getting back to Merrick's was going to be work because how was Bryce supposed to remember traffic laws with the tip of a plug teased against his prostate and a load's worth of cum tucked safely inside of him?

He did manage it, though, and when he walked into Merrick's apartment, his brother was awake in the living room, watercolor pad open on the coffee table and the handle of a paintbrush between his teeth.

"The prodigal brother returns," Merrick said, looking back at the dragon he was painting.

Holden kicked off his shoes and sat down on the couch, as far away from Merrick as possible, but it wasn't far enough.

"Where have you been?"

"Hmn?"

Merrick sniffed, swirling his paintbrush into a water cup that looked ready to be refilled. "Have you already found someone to fuck?" he asked, still not looking at Bryce. "You smell like you just got out of a shower, and whoever you're sleeping with uses the same soap as Holden, so it's a little off-putting."

Bryce choked on his spit, forcing himself to swallow down as much of his shock as he could, lest he draw Merrick's attention to his burning hot cheeks.

"I got a job," he said instead. "Bartending at a club in Pasadena. I met someone there and went back to his place for a bit."

It wasn't a lie, but it also wasn't the whole truth either.

Merrick filled in some orange lines on the intricate dragon scales, and Bryce, for the most part, was content to watch. He'd always envied his brother's artistic talent. His own brain simply didn't work that way, but he was glad for it. One less thing to be compared to Merrick about.

"Are you being safe?"

"Yeah, of course."

"Is it serious?" Merrick asked next.

"We barely know each other," he said, which was again not a lie but not the whole truth. There was no easy way to tell Merrick he'd fallen in love with Holden, especially since he'd barely been in town for a week and Merrick didn't even know Bryce had seen Holden outside of the first day he'd arrived. "I do like him, though."

Merrick ignored the last bit. "Where did you get a job at?"

"A place called Rapture."

That was apparently the magic word because Merrick set down his paintbrush and leveled an extremely judgmental and unimpressed look at him. "Do you know what that place is?"

"Do *you*?"

Merrick sniffed, eyes narrowing. They were clearly at an impasse, and Bryce had no interest in knowing why his brother knew about Rapture and what happened there. He could have lived his entire life not thinking about what Merrick did in the bedroom and died happy. The thought of Merrick knowing the things Bryce liked was almost enough to send him to an early grave anyway.

"You'll have to let me know what nights you work," was Merrick's answer, and it was quite an admission on its own.

"I will," he promised. "It's been a long day, though, so I think I'm going to bed."

"I won't be far behind you. Just trying to finish this up."

Bryce stood up and turned to go. He was halfway to the hallway when Merrick called after him, "I know you don't want to stay here long-term, but I'm glad you're here and you're welcome to the guest room as long as you want it."

It might have been the nicest thing Merrick had ever said to him, and he didn't know what to do with it.

"Do you want to get lunch soon?" he asked. "Or dinner or something."

"Maybe Sunday?" Merrick suggested, reaching again for his paintbrush.

"I have plans," Bryce said.

Merrick rolled his eyes. "We'll figure something out."

"Always have."

"Always will," his brother agreed.

Bryce waited to make sure Merrick didn't have anything else to say, then he locked himself in the guest room and stripped out of his suddenly too-tight clothes. He could feel his pulse in his ass for how horny he was, and he made quick work of setting his phone up on the nightstand and finding the right angle to give Holden the view he would want.

Bryce pressed record and assumed the position, teasing the plug out of him with a wet squelch. There was no quieting the moan that fell out of his throat, so he shoved his underwear into his mouth like a gag, giving the camera—and Holden—an imploring look before turning back around onto all fours. Bryce pushed until his hole relaxed and cum leaked down the back of his sac. He bit down hard around his makeshift gag and scooped up what he could catch on the sides of his fingers before thrusting it back into his hole.

God, he was so fucking hard and horny.

Holden had unlocked a visceral kind of want that Bryce had no interest in turning off. Maybe if he had a week, he could get some of it out of his system, but as he pushed a second finger into himself, cum sticking and smearing around his knuckles, he knew that was a lie. He would never get enough of Holden, but more than that, he didn't want to.

CHAPTER 15

Holden

THE DAYS DRAGGED ON, a series of one tattoo after another and another, all of it blurring into nights wrapped up in Bryce's long and trembling limbs. Holden and Bryce had fallen into a bit of a routine, but nothing that would arouse suspicion with Merrick, who still had no idea about the two of them. He certainly knew Bryce was seeing somebody. Holden had listened to Merrick whine about it at least once a day for the past two weeks, but he couldn't figure out who. It was a small relief for Holden to find out they'd been doing a good job at keeping their relationship under wraps.

And it was a relationship, after all. They were boyfriends.

Secret boyfriends.

Holden carried another secret, though. That he'd fallen in love with Bryce Shannon whether he'd meant to or not. Bryce promised he was just as all-in as Holden was, but Holden knew things were sometimes said in the heat of the moment. He wanted to trust it, because he did trust Bryce, but it was hard. Hannah told him more than once he was being ridiculous, that he would turn into a self-fulfilling prophecy if he didn't tell Bryce the truth, but he couldn't bring himself to do it. The moments they shared were as close to perfect as

Holden had ever imagined possible, and he wasn't ready to lose that yet.

"But what if it gets better?" Hannah had asked him last time they spoke.

He waved her off and said he had to get off the phone. She rolled her eyes at him but let the lie slide. It didn't matter; her question had been bouncing around in his head for days, and that was how he found himself at work early one Wednesday, bent over his sketchbook, tracing out a galaxy of constellations, Bryce's knuckle tattoos in the forefront of his mind.

Just before eleven, the upstairs door opened and the landing creaked. Holden set down his pencil and cracked his back, calling up to Riggs, "I'm in early."

The last thing he wanted was to catch his boss and his boss's boyfriend naked or in the middle of a sex thing, which was a real risk considering Riggs lived in the apartment over the shop. Smith had his own place in Hollywood, but he stayed over a lot. The two men were sickeningly in love, but Holden found it hopeful and inspiring.

Most of the time.

"I'm decent," Riggs announced, voice still thick with sleep. The stairs groaned as Riggs descended, and he blinked like an owl once he reached the bright lights of the shop. "Did you have an early appointment?"

"Just going stir crazy at home and wanted a change of scenery."

Riggs chuckled and tied his long hair up into a messy bun. "Most people would go to the beach or a coffee shop in that case, not work."

He gestured to Holden's empty chair. "Can I sit?"

"Your shop."

Holden rolled his stool back to make room for Riggs, who settled into the chair like a man who'd spent hours doing it. He had, in fact. Riggs was almost entirely covered in ink from his throat down to his ankles. Holden wasn't much further behind him as far as coverage went, but for some reason—maybe the hair and the constant five-o-clock shadow—Riggs looked a lot tougher than Holden ever would.

"What are you drawing? Do you mind sharing?"

Holden handed over his sketchbook. "Just stars."

Riggs smiled and tapped his finger against the corner of the page. "Can I flip?"

"There's no nudes in there, if that's what you're asking."

Riggs crossed his legs at the ankle and skimmed through Holden's sketchbook. It wasn't the first time. Holden had brought it with him for his interview, but Riggs had paid more attention to his finished portfolio than his in-process sketches. It made sense because the end product was what they were selling. Of course, it mattered how he got there, but that was the least of it.

"You are really good," Riggs finally said, handing the book back.

"You sound surprised."

"I wouldn't have hired you if you weren't," he said. "Just nice to be reminded, I think."

"Yeah, well. Thanks."

Riggs nodded and yawned, stretching his arms over his head. His shirt lifted, revealing a stripe of equally tattooed skin.

"How have you settled in here?" Riggs asked him. "You like it okay?"

"I like it a lot," he said. "I could stand for Merrick to talk less, but it's fine."

Riggs chuckled and nodded. "A man of many words, whereas you…"

"Are not."

A silence fell between them, and Holden fought the urge to fidget. It was nice, he realized, having Bryce around because their silences were never awkward, when they existed. Over their time together, Bryce had found the space to sit with himself long enough for Holden to find his own words. It made a special kind of peace in Holden's apartment that he wanted to carry with him always.

"Can I ask you something personal?" Riggs glanced up at the ceiling, a creaking floorboard that must have indicated his boyfriend was awake.

"If you had a human resources department, the answer would probably be no, but this is a tattoo shop, so sure."

"What do you do when you're not here?"

Holden laughed, scrubbing a hand down his face. HR or not, he absolutely could not answer that question truthfully. "Nothing exciting," he said.

"Are you seeing anyone? Do you date?"

Holden's heart lodged in his throat, and he tried to shrug off Riggs's question like he'd asked something much simpler like, "How's the weather?"

"I...sometimes."

"I know that's probably really out of line. Nothing I would have asked a year ago, but I wouldn't have had employees then either."

"Times change," Holden muttered.

Riggs nodded a thoughtful agreement. "I've learned lately that it's nice to have other people around. I've also seen how Merrick's brother looks at you when he comes into the shop."

Holden schooled his expression, licked his lips. "What do you mean?"

"He definitely thinks you're attractive. I don't know if you like men—"

"I do," he interrupted, grimacing at how loud his answer was. "I do. I mean, I like both."

"Merrick's brother is new in town. He looks a bit like a lost puppy when he comes by the shop."

He looked a bit like a debauched whore with his ass up and cum dripping down the backs of his thighs, but Bryce would be glad to know Riggs's opinion of him remained unfazed.

"He seems sweet," Holden managed to say.

"Sweet."

Holden glanced up from his sketchbook, finding Riggs's stare locked onto him, dark and curious.

"Okay," Riggs said, slapping the tops of his thighs and standing up.

Holden slid his stool out of the way to make room for his boss, all while doing everything he could to avoid Riggs's stare.

"I'd like to get on your books sometime."

"Pardon?"

"I want to get tattooed by you. I don't have a lot of room, but something small, I think." Riggs lifted his shirt revealing a small gap of skin on his ribs, not more than a three by two square.

"What did you want?"

"Dealer's choice," he said. "Just tell me when."

"Do you want to do it now?"

Riggs raised his brows, glancing at the clock on the wall over the door. It was an hour before the shop opened, an hour before Merrick arrived, and Holden didn't have an appointment until one.

"How long do you need?"

"We can knock it out before twelve."

"Alright." A huge smile split Riggs's face. "Let me tell Smith I'll be down here, and you can get set up."

Holden nodded and dropped his sketchbook onto the empty chair. He had no idea what to do in the small swatch of skin Riggs allocated for him, but he knew it needed to be good. Most of Riggs's work was black and gray, and there was no way Holden was going to do the same with the skin he'd been allowed. He flipped through his sketchbook, past the pages Riggs had inspected earlier, until he found a small snake he'd done, except the body of the animal was twisted into the shape of a heart, fangs dripping with venom. It was a decidedly new school take on an old school tattoo, and he could pack so much red and yellow into the scales that it would really pop in the dark shadows of Riggs's ribs.

He'd just finished setting up by the time Riggs came back downstairs. Coffee in hand, his boss sank down into the open chair and tugged his shirt to his armpit. "Is this good?"

"Yeah, totally, but sit up so I can get the stencil on."

Riggs shifted around and held his arm up, and an immense wash of pleasure rolled through Holden when he realized the stencil fit perfectly in the space allowed.

"What do you think?"

"Love it." Riggs settled back down into the chair and rested his head on his forearm. "Why a heart snake?"

"Well, I'd started sketching an ouroboros, and I was thinking about how they represent the never-ending cycles of life." Holden snapped on his gloves and tested the power to his machine before dipping the needle into a cup of black ink. He situated himself over Riggs and stretched the skin across his ribs, "Do you want a short line as a tester to remember how much this fucking sucks?"

Riggs laughed and shook his head. "Do your worst."

"I'll do my best," he offered instead, sinking a long and curved line into Riggs's skin. "But anyway, I was thinking about the forever nature of it and love felt like a forever thing too, so I tweaked the shape."

"Have you ever been in love?"

Holden wiped the ink away and laid a couple more lines before he answered, lip pinched between his teeth in concentration.

"Sorry," Riggs said when the buzzing of Holden's machine went quiet. "You've talked to me more today than you have in the past seven months, I think. I don't want to overdo it."

Holden exhaled a breath that sounded a lot like a laugh and paid attention to the tattoo, appreciating the quiet Riggs was offering him. There was something sacred about being in a tattoo shop on either side of the needle. There were lots of people, Holden included, who got tattoos because they were silly or because they had too much time and not enough sense, but there were also people who got tattoos that mattered. Holden had done dozens if not hundreds of memorial tattoos, doing his best to pretend he didn't see his clients crying through the process. He'd done complicated pieces that had taken him hours to sketch, a hodgepodge of ideas that all meant so much to the recipient that they couldn't narrow it down to a single thing. Tattoos were real and they were serious, and maybe it was his appreciation for the art and the commitment that always sent him into such a space of quiet contemplation.

"I have been in love," Holden said after he'd finished the line work and the black shading. "I am in love."

It felt good to say it out loud, to admit this thing with Bryce was more than just raunchy sex. It absolutely was also raunchy sex, but there was something else underneath it that kept the two of them coming back to each other, drawn close like magnets desperate to connect. Holden realized he needed to be honest with Bryce about how he felt. Both of them deserved the truth. Both of them deserved to sit with their love, even if they had to sit in secret.

He had no illusions that telling Merrick would be an easy thing, but that could be a problem for the future. Besides, who was Merrick to argue about his brother's happiness if his brother was in love? Fuck, what if Bryce didn't love him back? No. That was impossible. Holden was creative, but he wasn't delirious. He knew the feelings went both ways, and he promised to be truthful about them.

Honest with himself.

Honest with Bryce.

"What's their name?" Riggs asked.

Holden glanced up, and Riggs rolled his eyes when Holden said nothing, settling back down into the chair and staring at the wall with a soft smirk on his face. He finished the tattoo in fifteen minutes, the color going in solid and easy. After he was done, he cleaned the piece, took a picture of it for his portfolio, and bandaged his boss with plastic wrap and medical tape. Riggs poked the gauze tape, the unspoken taunt the same as the verbal one Merrick often threw at him.

"Do you need me to tell you how to take care of it?" Holden teased, pulling off his gloves and flinging them into the trash.

"Unwrap it immediately and wash it with scented dish soap," Riggs shot back.

Holden laughed. "Just like that. Let me know how it heals up for you."

Riggs checked himself out in the mirror, the bright red and yellow scales visible even through the plastic wrap. It was a gorgeous pop of color in the darkness of Riggs's rib piece, and Holden was honored to fill the space.

"Thank you for this," Riggs said, letting his shirt fall. "How much do I owe you?"

"You don't," Holden promised. "The honor and the conversation were more than enough."

CHAPTER 16
Bryce

"YOU LOOK like you're in love," Verity said, leaning against the bar at Rapture and staring at the wall of bottles instead of Bryce. Verity was the co-owner of Rapture, alongside their best friend, Landon. Whereas Landon was stoic and practical in most things, unless his husband was around, Verity was like a walking dream. Non-binary, unintentionally androgynous, and utterly breathtaking, there wasn't a single room Bryce found that wasn't made better by their presence in some way.

Bryce had worked at Rapture for eight shifts over the last two weeks, and Verity had been around for most of them. They were as much a fixture as the towering stained glass panels on the outside walls, and Bryce had enjoyed watching the way people naturally gravitated toward them.

"That obvious?" he asked, which earned him a melodic laugh.

"I recognize the signs. You look just like Aaron."

Bryce finished rinsing a pint glass, looking up at Verity from the corner of his eye. "Is your husband so hopeless for you?"

"Of course he is," Verity teased. "He wouldn't be my husband if he wasn't."

Bryce groaned, nodding his agreement. "I haven't told him. Not Aaron, but…haven't told him I love him."

"What on earth are you waiting for?"

Bryce shrugged, moving on from washing to cutting limes. There was still half an hour before the club opened, and he had plenty of time to get the bar prepped.

"We haven't been together long. Also, I'm staying with my brother right now, and I don't think he would like it."

"Why does your brother's opinion matter?"

"He's my brother," Bryce answered. "Why wouldn't it?"

"I think it's one thing to take it into consideration, another thing to let it color your decision making," Verity said gently.

"They work together." Bryce shoved the sliced limes into the condiment tray, then refilled the cherries from the jar under the bar. After he finished, he wiped the bar top clean and shoved the towel into his back pocket.

"Do they have to stop working together if you're in a relationship with…" Verity trailed off, swirling their hand in the air.

"Holden."

"Do they have to stop working together if you're in a relationship with Holden?"

"No. I just don't want it to be weird."

"You're very sweet, Bryce, but you're very young. Too young to worry so much about other people."

"Verity!" Landon stuck his head out from the back hallway that housed his office. "Do you have a sec?"

"Always for you." Verity looked at Bryce, cocking their head to the side and giving him a silent appraisal. "Much too young."

Bryce made a dismissive sound in the back of this throat and said goodbye to his second boss. Well, technically his second. Maybe his third. Rapture was a lot like family, owned by two best friends and staffed by the kind of people who were in group chats and shared alarm codes. The lead bartender, a man named Callum, was also married to a friend of Landon's. The other senior bartender was in a relationship with Verity's brother, and it seemed Callum's boyfriend and Verity's brother were the only ones not employed by the club.

It was nice, Bryce had told Merrick and Holden—separately of course—to be in a place that felt so much like home. It made the adjustment of his move a lot easier. But Holden had a big part in that too. The two of them had come so close to admitting things that probably should have had no place in a relationship as new as theirs, but there was no denying how right it all felt when Bryce thought about saying the words.

He'd wanted Holden from the moment they'd seen each other. That walk to the sandwich shop had been torture, Holden's quiet flirting not making things any easier for him. Their first night together had been groundbreaking for him, and things hadn't slowed down since. Maybe it was fast to get tested, to commit as quickly as they had, but there was no denying how right it felt. Bryce had been with Bella for years, and he'd never felt for her the things he felt for Holden, and definitely nowhere near the level of intensity.

The past two weeks since he started the job at Rapture had passed in a bit of a blur. He'd seen Holden as much as he could, but not getting off until three in the morning on the weekends meant their time was short. They stole some overnights during the week, but it was hard with Bryce still using Merrick's car.

Which was precisely why a vehicle of his own was at the top of his to-do list. He'd come into work a little early to get the prep done because he was supposed to meet a guy who had a beater he was trying to sell for five grand. It was a bit more than Bryce wanted to spend, but he didn't want to waste money on something that wasn't reliable. Between the tips he'd made at Rapture and the money he had saved from home, it wouldn't make too huge of a dent in his savings.

His phone vibrated against his thigh, and he pulled it out to find a text from the car guy and a message from Holden. As much as he wanted to read it, he needed to take care of the car before Rapture opened. He ran out to the parking lot, taking the front stairs two at a time until he landed in the dirt in front of an idling early 2000s BMW 3 series. Even in the fading light of the day, he could tell there were some scratches and dings on the door panels, but that was fine with him as long as the car ran well.

Bryce gave the car a good once-over, test drove it around the block, then paid cash and took the title and the keys. It was quick and painless, and he snapped a picture of the black car beneath the parking lot lights and texted it to his brother.

YOU'VE GOT YOUR CAR BACK FINALLY.
MERRICK

Thank god. Is the apt next?

jkjk you know you're welcome to stay

I know but also yes.

After that, he jogged back into work, checking the message from Holden.

HOLDEN

When can I see you again?

It was such a simple question but also so loaded. Merrick had done a very good job at pretending to keep his nose out of Bryce's business, but it was only a matter of time before his brother got insistent, demanding more transparency about Bryce's whereabouts than he was willing to give. It wasn't necessarily a bad thing. Merrick had always been a little over-bearing, and Bryce knew he meant well. Bryce also hated lying, but he wasn't ready to out his secret relationship until he was certain it would last.

Tomorrow?

after tonight I'm off until Tuesday

Tonight

It'll be late and I don't have clothes.

He wanted to.
God, he wanted to.

I want to see you

come get a drink then

He slid his phone back into his pocket, ready for work, trying to pretend he wasn't about to jump out of his skin at the prospect of seeing Holden again. Verity had been right—it was so fucking obvious. How embarrassing.

Holden showed up two hours later, hair wet from a shower. Bryce saw him walk in and watched him snake his way through the dance floor before stepping up to the bar and waiting his turn. Bryce was in the middle of making margaritas for a group of four, and he smiled at Holden and stabbed the button on the blender. Blended drinks were an abomination, and he had no respect for anyone who ordered them outside of a restaurant setting, and even then...

Bryce finished pouring them out, took a heavy black credit card out of a twink's hand and started them a tab. He grabbed two beers for a couple on his way down to Holden and then finally, finally reached his man.

"Drink?" he asked, hating how giddy he felt in Holden's presence.

Holden's bright blue eyes searched his face and a soft smile flickered across his mouth. "I'll have a beer."

Bryce grabbed him one, popped the top, and slid the beer across the bar. Holden took it, raised it in a one-sided toast, then cocked his head to the side and smirked.

"I'm going to wander," Holden said. "Get some ideas."

Heat rolled down the length of Bryce's spine and he managed a nod, watching Holden take a sip of his beer before turning and heading back into the middle of the dance floor.

"So, that's Holden," Verity said in his ear, startling him.

Bryce jumped, hand flying up to his chest to keep his heart behind his sternum. "How did you know?"

"The heart eyes, probably."

"God." Bryce scrubbed a hand down his face. "Am I that bad?"

Verity reached up and tweaked the tip of Bryce's nose. "It's cute."

Bryce rolled his eyes. "It feels like it's killing me."

"Only because you're keeping it inside." Verity glanced toward the far wall of the club, and Bryce let his stare follow. He watched Holden climb the stairs, muscles flexing under the tight stretch of his plain white shirt. "For what it's worth, the feeling *is* mutual."

"How can you tell?"

Holden reached the loft and looked down at the bar, smiling when he caught Bryce and Verity staring up at him.

"He looks at you the same way."

"Does he?"

Holden finally looked away and Bryce let go of a breath he'd been holding.

"Does he?" Verity mocked. "Be serious."

Thankfully, before Bryce could come up with a response, a handsome man in a suit walked up to the bar. He ordered three drinks and carried them all away, up to the loft and into the dark. Bryce rested his elbows against the bar and groaned, unable to pick Holden's silhouette out of the shadows.

The night dragged on, and an hour later, Holden reappeared. His hair had finally dried and he walked downstairs slowly. Bryce watched as he made his way to the bar, setting down his empty beer bottle and pushing it toward Bryce.

"Another?" Bryce asked.

"I think one's good. I want my wits about me later."

"Why's that?"

Holden's lips quirked up at the corners. "I've got plans."

"Is that so?"

"Yeah. They're going to keep me busy until Monday night at the earliest, so I don't want to spend half that time hungover and hating life."

Bryce swallowed hard, tongue sticking to the roof of his mouth. "Monday?"

"If that works for you."

"It very much works for me," Bryce said.

Holden pulled a ten-dollar bill out of his wallet and set it down beside his beer bottle.

"Your brother won't worry about your whereabouts?"

"He'll assume the worst, which for him means I'm shacked up in a hotel with a married man or five."

Holden's expression darkened. "I don't like the way he thinks about you. The way he sees you."

Bryce thought about the conversation he'd had with his brother a couple of weeks before, when he'd gotten the job and told Merrick where he'd be working. It was hard for Bryce to reconcile his understanding of his brother with a version of the man he didn't know. The mere thought of Merrick enjoying time at Rapture was something impossible for Bryce to comprehend, and he imagined it was much the same for Merrick to do to him. There was so much about each other they didn't know anymore. Maybe that had been unintentional or maybe it had been by design—they were too many years into their lives for Bryce to know for sure—but it cost him nothing to ignore the digs his brother made about his sex life and his enjoyment of it.

"He's just projecting," Bryce said without having any idea about what Merrick said about him when he wasn't around. "Whatever he thinks about me doesn't bother me at all, so don't let it bother you."

Holden studied his face carefully, obviously searching for any indication Bryce wasn't being honest. He was being absolutely truthful about Merrick. There wasn't anything his brother said in public that he hadn't implied in private.

"I'll see you after work then?" Holden asked. "Mine until Monday?"

Yours until forever, Bryce thought.

"Until Monday."

CHAPTER 17
Holden

WHEN BRYCE SHOWED up after work, he was too tired to do anything besides collapse into Holden's arms and go to sleep. Holden didn't mind. He took Bryce to bed, stripped off his clothes, and held him until his breathing turned steady and slow. Holden fell asleep soon after and woke the next morning with their positions reversed with Bryce's face buried in the back of his neck and Bryce's fingers drawing lazy swirls across his chest.

"I like waking up with you," Holden said, half the words lost on a yawn. He rolled onto his back and Bryce tucked in against his ribs, cheek pillowed on Holden's chest.

"I like it too."

Holden stroked his fingers through Bryce's hair, pressing a kiss against the top of his head. They lay together in a comfortable silence, the sound of cars outside the window and annoying birds chirping on the roof the only sounds besides their level and even breaths. They'd talked about being boyfriends, which to Holden had always felt like such a trivial word for the kind of commitment he wanted to give someone. Boyfriends felt like it was a high school thing, a label kids used when they didn't know better or didn't care.

The way he felt for Bryce, even so soon after meeting, was far more monumental than "boyfriend" allowed, but Holden wasn't sure how to express that. Even in the space they'd built together where words weren't always necessary, Holden didn't know how to express the level of adoration he felt for Bryce, the level of want.

Need.

"For as quiet as you are," Bryce murmured, breath hot against Holden's nipple. "You sure think loud."

Holden made an amused sound and inhaled so deeply it raised Bryce's body.

"What are you thinking about?" Bryce asked next, clearly ready to use his words until Holden grew weary of it and took them away.

Holden arched a brow, and Bryce shoved off of him, pushing into a seated position with the sheets pooled in his lap and his knee digging into Holden's side.

"What are you thinking about?" Holden countered.

"I'm thinking about how long I can make it before the anticipation of you pumping me full of fake cum kills me." Bryce grinned, cheeks pink in the late morning light. "But I'm also thinking about how if that never happens, it would be perfectly okay."

Holden thought of the bag of supplies in his nightstand. "It'll happen," he promised.

Bryce's lashes fluttered a little. "I'm really lucky to have found you, I think."

Something constricted in Holden's chest, and he danced his fingertips across Bryce's hip, easing the sheet down until Bryce's thigh was visible. Holden had always been so eager to bed the other man he'd never paid attention to Bryce's tattoos. At least not beyond the stardust on his knuckles. Bryce's body was a dedication to his brother, a portfolio of Merrick's tattoos scattered across his skin.

"Now tell me what you're thinking about," Bryce said.

"I'm thinking about how I'd secretly worried talking all night at work would make you tired of it by the time you came home to me."

The air crackled, and Bryce worried his lower lip between his teeth. Holden had used a lot of honest words in that sentence, but maybe not in the ideal order. He was very close to showing his hand.

"Worried?" Of course Bryce picked up on that. "You were worried I'd come back here after work and have nothing to say to you?"

Holden opened his mouth to argue, but Bryce showed no signs of stopping.

"And *come home to you?*" He flung one leg over Holden's body and straddled him, fingers steepled on Holden's chest. He ground his hips down against him, both of them shivering from the friction. "I think you like me, Holden Walker."

Holden grabbed his hips, stilled him.

"I do," he rasped, searching Bryce's face for any trepidation or distaste at his very understated two-word confession.

What he got instead was a bright smile and a soft laugh.

"I like you too. And don't worry, I'll always have something to say to you."

"Unfortunate," Holden teased, and Bryce's smile somehow grew wider. Bryce opened his mouth, but something flashed across his face and he snapped his mouth closed, licking his lips like he wanted to seal them closed.

"What?" Holden prompted.

"Nothing."

"Not like you to keep something back."

Bryce huffed out a laugh and lifted one shoulder to his ear in a casual shrug. "Last night at the bar, you said you had plans for me, but the only thing we did was go to sleep."

Holden was fairly certain that wasn't what Bryce had been about to say, but he'd come up with a way to get the truth out of him later. Or he could probably wait it out. Bryce still wasn't a fan of the silence, and he rattled on more often than not, especially if he was horny. Maybe it was some kind of Pavlovian response Holden had trained into him by accident that if he talked too much, Holden would fuck him back to silence.

"You were very tired," Holden said. "And I have you until Monday so there is plenty of time."

"Not if I die first."

Bryce gave him puppy dog eyes, and Holden flattened his hands against the small of Bryce's back and used him for leverage to sit up. Bryce jostled in his lap, the weight shifting on Holden's half-awake cock. The way his dick twitched didn't go unnoticed, and Bryce smirked like he'd just won a scavenger hunt.

"I'm horny," Bryce whined.

"You can wait."

"I don't want to."

Holden realized in that moment, he never wanted to tell Bryce no. About anything. He wanted to give Bryce everything he wanted, whether that was a dick to suck or a quiet hour of respite from the endless stream of noise in his mind. That was so much more serious than the word boyfriend allowed, but they'd only known each other a handful of weeks and how could he admit any of that out loud? He found himself jealous of Bryce's gift of talk, wishing it came easier for him because maybe then he could be honest with them both about what he really wanted.

"I don't care," Holden said softly, stroking his thumbs across Bryce's cheeks.

Bryce's breath stuttered out of him, the denial clearly just as arousing as when Holden gave in to him.

"I want to get dressed, and I want to take you to lunch. I want to spend the day with you outside of my apartment."

There was an implication with the statement that he wanted Bryce for more than sex.

"Like a date?"

"Maybe."

"That is something boyfriends do, I suppose."

Holden scrunched his nose. There was that fucking word again.

"No?" Bryce asked, lip pushed out into a frown.

"Yes," Holden agreed. "It's something boyfriends do."

"What else?"

"I just want to waste some time with you," he admitted.

Bryce hummed, taking Holden's face into his hands and bringing their noses together, their mouths. He paused, and Holden knew it was because he'd already said no to sex. This was Bryce asking for permission to take what he wanted, even if ran counter to what Holden had expressed. But Holden had no issues with a kiss. A kiss was…he would have kissed Bryce every second of the day. But he would have fucked him too, and he'd put a stop to that because he wanted more. A kiss would be okay, though, as long as he could stop himself.

He closed the very small space between them and pressed his mouth against Bryce's. His concession rewarded him with the slide of Bryce's arms around his neck and a moan that went right to Holden's cock. He licked into Bryce's mouth, grabbing the back of Bryce's neck to keep him still so he could control the kiss. Bryce seemed to have no issue letting Holden lead, even as his hips started to move. The hot line of Bryce's cock against his stomach was enough to make him stop, and he tore himself away with a gasp, pressing their foreheads together.

Holden could see his spit on Bryce's lips. "You're a siren," he murmured.

"I don't think I'll ever apologize for making you want to fuck me."

Holden squeezed the back of Bryce's neck. "I want to do more than fuck you."

Bryce's tongue stuck to the roof of his mouth, making a soft clicking sound as he pulled it free. He leaned back and studied Holden, and Holden held his breath, not sure what Bryce saw when he looked at him.

"Oh," Bryce said quietly.

"Oh?"

"*Oh*," he said again, this time with more emphasis. "I see it now."

"See what?"

"Verity knew who you were at the bar last night before I'd told them your name," Bryce explained. "Knew you were the man I…knew you were my boyfriend."

Holden briefly entertained the idea of striking the word boyfriend from Bryce's vocabulary, but he didn't have anything better to replace it with.

Yet.

"How did they know that?" he asked.

"The way you look at me," Bryce whispered.

Holden licked his lips, heart slamming violently against his sternum. "How do I look at you?"

Bryce laughed at him, crawling off Holden's lap and dragging him out of bed. He stumbled after Bryce until they were both in the bathroom. Bryce flipped the lights on and stood with his back against the counter so Holden faced him and the mirror.

"Look at me," Bryce said, and Holden did.

Because of course he did.

He studied the dark pools of Bryce's eyes and the soft swell of his cheeks and the plush lines of his mouth. Holden traced his fingers over the hint of scruff growing out against Bryce's jaw, the small diamond tattoo in front of his ear.

"Now look at you," Bryce instructed and Holden flickered his stare to the mirror.

It was quick, his expression changing when he became his focus instead of Bryce, but it was there for a moment…the thing Bryce saw when Holden looked at him. What Verity saw. What everyone must have seen.

"Bryce, I—"

"I think I love you," Bryce blurted before Holden could say anything else. "I'm not sure because I thought I loved Bella, but it didn't feel anything like this. I don't know if it's just the sex hormones or—"

"It's not," Holden cut him off, fingers pressed against Bryce's still moving lips. "It's not just the hormones."

"I love you?"

Holden laughed under his breath, tracing his finger across Bryce's lower lip before moving his fingers to Bryce's chin.

"Are you not sure?" he asked.

"No." A violent flush colored Bryce's cheeks and he tucked his chin toward his chest to escape Holden's stare. "I'm not."

Something constricted, tightening every muscle in his body like he was a rubber band ready to snap. Holden tilted Bryce's face back up and looked at him again. He didn't even have to try to morph his features into what Bryce had seen before. It was impossible, he realized, to look at Bryce and not let his emotions through.

Holden leaned in slowly and ghosted a kiss across the corner of Bryce's mouth. Bryce chased after him, hungry and urgent, and the kiss quickly turned into something that was going to lead them, again, right back to bed. Holden had to take Bryce's face into his hands and pull their mouths apart, and even then Bryce chased after his mouth.

"Oh," Bryce murmured, lashes fluttering.

"Oh," Holden agreed, knowing he loved Bryce and knowing it was returned.

CHAPTER 18

Bryce

BRYCE REALIZED, after getting dressed and brushing his teeth beside Holden at his small bathroom sink, he'd never actually been in love before. He watched Holden's reflection in the mirror, the way his hair fell into his eyes when he leaned over to spit out the toothpaste, the way he wiped his mouth with the back of his hand. There wasn't a single thing Holden did that Bryce didn't want to worship, and that scared him a little.

Was love supposed to be scary?

He wasn't sure.

Even with his nerves and worry over the confession of their feelings—even unspoken—there was a safety in it, which only proved to Bryce he was right in the first place. He didn't know if love was supposed to be scary, but it definitely was supposed to feel safe, and Bryce had never felt more protected than he did when he was with Holden.

"I can drive," he offered after they put their shoes on.

"Ah, yes." Holden stood up and shook himself into shape. "The new car. Let's see it."

Holden took Bryce's hand after he locked the apartment, and there was something so freeing about it. He'd never *wasted a day* with anyone before, but he was ready for Holden to be his first. In many things, apparently. Down on the street, Bryce unlocked the car and Holden gave the BMW a quick appraisal before pulling open the passenger door and sinking into the black leather seat.

"What do you think?" Bryce asked.

"It's nice."

"I thought so." He turned the car on and unrolled the windows to let some fresh air in. The car smelled a little bit like weed even though Bryce didn't smoke. "Where is our first stop?"

Holden plugged an address into the nav and then reached over the console to take Bryce's hand. Even without using his words, Holden said *so much* sometimes Bryce found it over-whelming...in the best way. In the *he wanted more of it* way.

Whatever place Holden had decided on for lunch was just over half an hour away, and the directions called for him to go west, so that's where Bryce headed. He turned on the radio, enjoying the feel of Holden's hand in his while he drove. Holden didn't say much, but when Bryce asked him questions, he answered. By the time they reached Santa Monica, Bryce knew how long Holden had been tattooing for, what his favorite movie was, what he liked to do in his spare time when he wasn't barebacking Bryce, and a slew of other inconsequential facts. He'd offered all of his own answers to Holden in return, who nodded quietly with a smile on his face.

"Noted," Holden murmured, tapping his temple after Bryce pulled into a metered spot a few blocks from the beach. "Where are we going?"

The two of them got out of the car and Holden took his hand again, squeezing his fingers before leading him a couple blocks away from the beach toward a little taco shop that wasn't much more than a hole in the wall with a sliding window and a menu on a folding easel board.

"What is it with you and places like this?" Bryce teased, thinking back to the cafe around the corner from Ink and Ember Merrick had sent them to his first day in LA. That hadn't been too long ago, but it felt like a lifetime. How had Bryce met—and fallen in love with—someone in such a short amount of time?

"I know what I like."

Bryce hummed. "You certainly do."

They stood quietly together in line, and Bryce leaned his head against the outside of Holden's shoulder. It was nice, he thought, finding the quiet outside of the bedroom. To Bryce, it was more proof he'd chosen right, that Holden's love was as safe as he thought it was.

When it was their turn in line, Holden ordered for him and Bryce continued to relax. His shoulders sagged, his fingers softened in Holden's grip. He wasn't trying to pull away, but he trusted Holden's feelings for him and also didn't feel like he needed to hold on so hard. So much of his life with Merrick had been a fight for attention, for love, for resources. With Holden, everything he offered was freely given with no moderation in sight. Holden gave and gave and gave to him, and Bryce had never been able to take so freely. He knew his relationship with Holden couldn't stay a secret forever, but he would be lying if he said he didn't want this to himself for just a little longer.

Ten minutes later, Holden grabbed a brown paper bag with a dozen street tacos inside of it, took Bryce's hand again, and led them back toward PCH. Bryce didn't say how happy it made him to let Holden take the lead. He didn't think he had to.

They made their way to the short concrete wall of the boardwalk and both of them sat down, the food between them. Bryce watched quietly as Holden meticulously pulled out all the tacos and arranged them on top of the bag.

"Are you going to feed me too?" he joked, grabbing one of the foil-wrapped tacos and tearing into it.

The scent of marinated pork and pineapple wafted up to his nose and Bryce made an indecent sound when he breathed it in. Holden shot him a scathing look, his own taco in hand.

"Save it for later," Holden muttered.

Bryce laughed and took another bite of his taco. It really was delicious and well worth the drive to Venice. Behind them, people skated and jogged down the boardwalk, and before them, the waves crashed onto the shore. There was so much noise, so much happening around them, but it was just him and Holden. The two of them in a little bubble that apparently could extend past the bedroom.

They ate all twelve tacos, and then Bryce took care of the trash before Holden could get up. When he came back to the wall, Holden pulled him close, one arm around his waist and the outsides of their legs touching.

"I could get used to this," Bryce said softly, closing his eyes and enjoying the warmth as the sun beat down on the top of his head.

"The beach?"

"You."

Holden's fingers flexed against his side. "I didn't tell you earlier, but—"

Holden was interrupted before he could get the words out. What Bryce imagined would have been Holden's first time using the L-word with him instead turned into the sound of Merrick saying Holden's name.

Holden's fingers twitched against him again, and he moved to pull his arm back. Bryce didn't stop him, and neither of them dared to breathe. So much for his little bubble of peace with Holden, so much for their secret.

"Bryce?" His own name fell out of his brother's mouth

with much more surprise than he'd offered Holden's. "What are you two doing here?"

"Merrick." Bryce climbed off the wall and brushed sand off the backs of his thighs. Holden stayed seated, expression watchful.

"What's going on? You two looked—"

"Close," Bryce offered.

"Close."

Merrick's eyes narrowed, and he looked from Bryce to Holden and back again. Merrick was on a longboard, a paper bag that looked a lot like the one Bryce had just thrown away in his hand.

"Holden?" Merrick asked, and Holden glanced up, shoulders heaving with a deep inhale.

"Merrick."

"What are you two doing here?"

Bryce's brother had apparently turned his attention to Holden after not getting the answer he wanted out of Bryce himself.

"Having lunch," Holden answered.

"And a snuggle?"

"Hardly."

"It looked close."

"I told you it was," Bryce interjected.

Merrick's gaze drifted back to his brother. "You've been staying with him, haven't you?"

Holden swung his leg over the wall and stood beside Bryce, shoulder to shoulder. He stared down Bryce's brother like he would fight the man if he had to, but Bryce knew it wouldn't come to that.

"He has," Holden answered, brushing his fingers against Bryce's. A shiver of already familiar electricity coursed up his arm, raising the hair up to his elbow.

Something that looked a lot like hurt flashed across Merrick's face and his stare drifted back to Bryce.

"You didn't say anything," Merrick said.

And in that moment, Bryce felt bad about not telling his brother about his relationship with Holden, but he wasn't going to apologize for wanting something for himself.

"I know," Bryce said. He tangled his fingers with Holden's and held on for dear life. "And I don't want to talk about it now. Can we do this later?"

For the first time in his entire life, Bryce saw his brother at a loss for words.

"Later." Merrick rubbed the bridge of his nose, dragging his finger over to rub his eye.

"We can talk at work," Holden said. "If you want."

"Oh, I'll want." Merrick seemed to remember himself, squaring his shoulders and squinting at Holden. Bryce didn't see any malice in the look, though, just weariness.

"It wasn't about you," Holden added. "For what it's worth."

Merrick swallowed hard and nodded. "Heard."

"We'll talk soon, I promise," Bryce said. "I love you."

Holden squeezed his hand and Merrick jerked his chin in agreement with the sentiment. Bryce and Merrick looked at each other for another beat, then Merrick turned forward again on his longboard and skated toward the pier. Once his back disappeared into the crowd, Bryce let out a breath and smashed his face against Holden's chest.

Holden was quick to embrace him, wrapping both arms around Bryce's shoulders and pulling him in for a much-needed hug. Bryce breathed in the calming smell of Holden's laundry detergent and his body wash, counting his breaths until he felt like he could speak without his heart jumping out of his throat.

"I'm proud of you, if that's not weird to say," Holden whispered into his hair.

"Why?"

"You said what you needed to say, and you didn't run out of breath while doing it."

Bryce wiggled out of Holden's arms enough to see his face, relief trickling down his spine when he saw the soft smile on Holden's mouth. Holden took Bryce's face into his hands and pressed a gentle kiss against his mouth, a little rougher than would be considered polite, but nowhere near aggressive enough to be considered inappropriate.

"I love you," Holden said, kissing the corner of Bryce's mouth, his chin, the cut of his jaw. Bryce tilted his head back to give Holden his neck, which earned him a toothy grin against his skin but no more kisses.

"I love you," he shivered, laughing to himself. "I never would have thought."

"That you'd love me?"

"That it would feel like this." Bryce tucked his chin against his chest and shrugged awkwardly. "This may not be doable because Merrick has always been able to kill the mood, but did you have anything else planned for the day?"

Holden arched a brow, the insinuation clear. He thought Bryce was chasing after when they were going to go back home and fuck, which wasn't entirely wrong but was also honestly not the root of his question. Holden had asked him to waste a day, and Bryce was committed to doing exactly that.

"I was going to see where the mood took us," Holden said. "I didn't have anything concrete until tonight."

Bryce made an awkwardly horny sound. Holden laughed and joined their hands again and pulled Bryce back toward where they'd parked. "You're insatiable," he teased.

"Can you blame me?"

"Honestly, no." Holden's mouth quirked up into a little smile. "But you're going to have to wait for what you want. And you're probably going to have to wait longer than you want."

"It's already been longer than I want." Bryce covered their joined hands with his other hand, enjoying the contact. "Do you think if I talk long enough you'll give in because it'll be an opportunity to shut me up?"

"As much as I love when I can make you quiet, there's not much I love more than the sound of your voice, Bryce."

The admission slammed into him like a semi-truck. He rubbed his chest, trying to ease the ache and the pressure that love seemed to leave behind.

"Oh, well." He unlocked the car. "In that case, have I got a story for you."

CHAPTER 19

Holden

BRYCE WAS all nerves on the drive back to Holden's house. He didn't stop talking from the second the car turned on up until Holden got his key into the front door. Holden didn't stop him; he knew enough about Bryce by then to know it was a coping mechanism, especially when it came to his brother. Getting caught together hadn't been either of their plans, but life had a way and now they both were left to the deal with the consequences of being outed prematurely.

With the door closed and locked behind them, Holden toed off his sneakers and leaned against the wall with a heavy sigh. "Are you done?"

Bryce finished his sentence, shoulders sagging on a long exhale.

He went quiet so quickly, it made Holden's dick hard.

"Good," Holden told him. "Take some time in the bathroom to get ready, then come to bed. Okay?"

It was the middle of the day still, but Holden had no plans of coming up for air until the sun had set and risen again. There were enough snacks in his fridge to hold them over, and the sort of sex he had in mind was not ideal after a taco lunch, but Holden had faith it would all work out in the end.

He brushed Bryce's hair away from his forehead and kissed him.

"Okay," Bryce said softly.

Bryce shuffled into the bathroom and Holden waited until the shower turned on to set up the bed. He'd debated the merits of getting a hotel or something so he didn't have to deal with the mess their sex would leave behind, but in the end, he'd opted against it. Holden wanted his sheets stained, his lube empty. He wanted to remember what Bryce looked like on his bed, full to bursting and desperate for release.

He'd already remade his bed with a waterproof sheet beneath his normal fitted sheet, and he hoped that would be enough. Bryce's kink wasn't feeling it come out of him, it was keeping it in, and Holden wanted to make sure he did exactly that. While Bryce prepped himself in the bathroom, Holden made sure everything he needed was within reach, then he stripped down to his underwear and sat on the edge of the bed.

It wasn't a good idea, but Holden checked his phone while he waited. As expected, there was a text message from Merrick. He debated reading it or letting it go, but knowing the message was there and unread would distract him and he wanted to be completely focused on Bryce when he got out of the shower. Getting caught by Merrick on the beach had unsettled them both, Bryce especially. Holden didn't think Bryce had ever stood up to his brother in his entire life, but he'd done it there on the boardwalk, fingers dancing across the tops of Holden's knuckles.

He swiped to the message, finding a chunky text that required him to scroll to read the whole thing. Holden scoffed. It was the most stereotypically Merrick thing that could have possibly happened to him.

MERRICK

I'm not mad

Well, I am mad. But I'm not mad that you're sleeping with my brother. I'm mad you didn't tell me you were sleeping with my brother and I'm mad my brother didn't tell me he was sleeping with you. I thought he'd been out with randos or worse and he never told me otherwise and he's new to town and I didn't want him to get hurt. I don't think you'll hurt him, you don't seem like the type, but I don't think I know you well enough to decide one way or another. Bryce is a good judge of character, though, and I don't think Riggs would have hired you if you were shady, but that's all I have to go off right now so I am mad. I am mad, but I think all things considered, you're probably not a bad choice for him. He talks a lot and probably can't be with someone who talks a lot too and you never talk at all. How long has this been going on, by the way? It can't be since the first day he got into town?? Is it since then? I wish I had thought of all these questions when I saw you two on the beach, but I was so shocked to see either of you there, let alone seeing you together. Like TOGETHER together. I love my brother, and I want him to be happy. I don't think his ex made him happy. Has he told you about her? Probably, he talks a lot, but I don't think he was happy with her and I haven't seen him a lot since he moved down, but I hope he's happy with you. Anyway, I'm mad but also mad at myself that he didn't think he could tell me about you or that he didn't want to tell me. I don't know which is worse honestly. He's not mad at me, is he? Are you? Fuck, I hate this. Please don't wait too long to talk to me about this.

Holden read the message a few times, picking up something new on every pass. Merrick's brain was a wild place, Holden realized. It took work to make Bryce look soft-spoken, but somehow Merrick managed to do it. Even with how much talking Bryce had done on the way home from the beach, he at least managed to stay on topic. Merrick was like a pinball machine, jumping from one idea to the other. It was enough to give Holden whiplash.

He texted Merrick back. *Everything is fine. Don't worry.*

Then he turned off his ringer and set his phone face down on the nightstand.

Fifteen minutes later, Bryce emerged from the bathroom with wet hair and a towel wrapped around his waist. His chest looked flushed and there was a growing bulge below the knot of the towel. Bryce looked at him sheepishly, standing a few feet away from the foot of the bed.

"Where do you want me?"

"Right there," he said. "I want you to drop the towel, and I want to watch you touch yourself."

Bryce loosened the knot and the towel fell to his feet. He was hard, like Holden had guessed, and Bryce wasted no time taking himself in hand and stroking his full length. Holden watched Bryce touch himself until his own dick was hard, then he angled his head toward the bed in invitation. Bryce made a show of crawling up from the bottom with his back arched and his ass in the air. He looked good enough to eat—and Holden planned to—but he was going to spend plenty of time making sure Bryce was ready for it first.

"Never in my life have I come as hard as I do when I'm inside of you," Holden whispered, situating himself behind Bryce and petting his hands over the swell of his ass cheeks. "It pours out of me like I'm made of nothing but pleasure meant to fill you up."

This was part of his plan. They both knew Holden had gone to the store and bought a bag of that fake cum, and they both knew he planned to get it into Bryce's body, but they hadn't discussed the intricacies of how that was going to happen. He had Bryce's consent for the act itself, but Holden hadn't thought it would be really sexy to simply funnel fake cum into Bryce until it leaked out of him. He wanted something more intimate, something that wouldn't take either of them out of the moment.

In the end, it had been easy to rig the bag with a thin enough tube he'd be able to get the end into Bryce's ass alongside his own cock. He'd be able to pump Bryce full of fake cum and real cum at the same time, riding out an orgasm with everything he wished his body could allow him to give.

"I want you."

"You have me."

Holden had hidden the bag under the blanket at the foot of the bed but he'd left the lube on top. He slicked his fingers and thrust them into Bryce's exposed hole, leaning down and adding his tongue to the mix. Holden gave himself permission to be loud in their silence, sucking and lapping at Bryce's rim. He swirled his tongue around his knuckles, scissoring his fingers open so he could lick the inside of Bryce's hole. Beneath him, Bryce pushed back, rubbing Holden with his ass. Holden dug his fingers into Bryce, twisting his wrist until he found Bryce's prostate. Bryce buried his face into the pillows and moaned, his entire body trembling when Holden got three fingers inside and against him. Bryce was so wet with lube, the sounds of Holden's hand working him open sounded more like a pussy than an asshole, and Holden had to rest his forehead against Bryce's ass to steady himself.

"It feels so good," Bryce whined when he went still. "Don't stop."

"I want this to last."

"I want you now."

"I want you to stop talking now," Holden said simply, and with a crackle, the air in the room changed. Bryce sucked in a shaky breath, his entire body relaxing at the statement. Holden could have gotten his whole hand into Bryce at that point, but that was another conversation and another game entirely.

Bryce was silent, and Holden lined his cock up and thrust inside.

Bryce did speak after that, a muttered curse before he bit the pillow between his teeth. His eyes rolled back as Holden started to move. He didn't plan for this to last long, he never could with Bryce, but he didn't want it to end before it even got going. Steeling himself against his own pleasure, he sank fully into Bryce's well-lubed hole. Bryce held him tight, and Holden reached around and grabbed Bryce's dick in his fist. He started to stroke him, slow and loose, working him toward an orgasm he had no plans on seeing through. He wanted Bryce trembling and desperate by the time he finished.

He pressed his chest over the curves of Bryce's back, kissing the nape of his neck and pulling them both into an awkward and tight seated position. He banded his arm around Bryce's chest to hold him steady and dragged his tongue up the side of Bryce's neck.

"Ride me," he whispered. "But don't come. And don't you dare make me come."

Bryce groaned, starting slow. Holden tightened his hand around Bryce's cock, knowing it wouldn't be long at all before his boyfriend was a sweaty and writhing mess on his lap. Holden bit the inside of his cheek and closed his eyes because watching Bryce move on top of him would have sent him flying over the edge and past the point of no return.

"You're so tight," he rasped, sliding his hand down and pinching Bryce's already hard nipple between his fingers. "So fucking hot."

"I'm close."

"Don't."

"I can't *stop it*," Bryce protested, his pace faltering.

His breath came in rough and staggered pants, and

Holden shoved him forward, pulling back and letting his cock slide free. It hurt to not be inside of Bryce anymore, but they were both perilously close to coming and Holden wanted to make it count. He teased the fingers of one hand over Bryce's swollen hole and aligned the tube of the cum bag along the top of his shaft. He'd picked one thick enough to not pinch closed, but thin enough that he hoped Bryce wouldn't feel it.

"You're gonna make me come harder than I've ever come in my life," he promised, and it was the actual truth. "I'm going to pump so much cum into you, it'll be leaking down your thighs for days."

Bryce's hips fucked the air, and he screwed his eyes closed like he was in pain. He fisted the sheets, the need to stroke his cock long forgotten.

Holden got himself and the tube inside, and he managed three short thrusts before heat began to crest at the base of his spine.

"Can you come with me?" he grunted, fingers of his left hand digging into Bryce's hip. "Come and milk it out of..."

Bryce did come, an agonized wail as his body tightened down on Holden and did exactly what he'd hoped it would. Holden came so hard he saw stars, and as his orgasm ripped through him, he tucked the bag under his arm and grabbed Bryce with both of his hands, thrusting even deeper than he had before.

"Fuck, Bryce. I'm still coming." His vision cleared, his breathing settled. "Oh fuck How am I still coming? I'm gonna fill you up with so much fucking cum. Oh, God. It won't stop. It won't fucking stop."

CHAPTER 20
Bryce

BRYCE'S ORGASM went on forever. He barely touched his dick before it spurted jets of sticky white cum across the tips of his fingers and the dark blue of Holden's sheets. Behind him, Holden groaned, hips still as he came.

And came.

And came.

A wet heat continued to pour into Bryce's ass, and a shiver tore through him when hot cum trickled out of him and dribbled down his sac and his shaft.

"So much fucking cum inside of you," Holden murmured, his hands releasing Bryce's hips and petting long and delicate lines over the arch of his back. "You're so fucking full, it's already leaking out of you and I've got so much more for you still."

Bryce's breathing stuttered as he realized what was happening, when he realized Holden was helping him live out one of his dirtiest fantasies. Holden's cock was still inside of him and Holden gave a slow thrust, the squelch of cum and lube louder than his own heartbeat. His stomach cramped and a familiar fullness overtook him. Bryce flattened his cheek against the sheets and reached back, feeling for the reassuring shape of Holden's body.

"Is that what you needed?" Holden whispered, finally easing himself out of Bryce's hole. His body gaped and chased after the sensation of being stuffed full of cock even as cum poured out of his ass for how much was inside of him. "Is that enough cum to fill you up?"

Holden reached around and gently pressed his fingertips against Bryce's stomach, barely distended. Bryce moaned, a violent shiver bursting out of him. The move was so sudden, more cum pooled around his puckered rim before leaking out of him and down the backs of his thighs.

"You're full of it," he said. "Full to bursting. You made me come so fucking hard."

Bryce closed his eyes, relishing the feeling of all the cum inside of him, the way his body ached for more of it even though he knew it was too much. Holden dragged his fingertips up the split of Bryce's ass, pushing two fingers in with embarrassing ease. Bryce moaned and thrashed, and Holden quieted him through it, pushing some of the escaped cum back into his body.

"God, you should see yourself." Holden groaned, a low and rumbling sound in the back of his throat. He withdrew his fingers from Bryce's hole and spread him open. "Show it to me. Show me your hole."

Bryce's entire body broke out in a cold sweat, gooseflesh peppering his arms as he bore down and pushed out to give Holden what he wanted. Holden made a pleased sound and then his mouth was there, tongue wet and hot against Bryce's insides.

"I fucking love you," Holden said next, pulling away and covering Bryce's swollen entrance with his hand. There was no stopping the constant dribble of cum that had already started to slide out of him, but Holden's hand there made

Bryce feel like it would stay in a little while longer, that the fantasy wasn't ready to be over yet.

"I love you," he rasped, sounding drunk even to his own ears.

"I want you again."

Holden lowered Bryce onto his side and fitted his body against Bryce's back. A cock nudged Bryce's ass and then Holden was inside of him again, thrusting long and slow, cum slicking his way. Bryce was so wet between his legs, so sticky, and Holden fucked into him like they had all the time in the world. Bryce shuddered, reaching back and grabbing Holden's hair in his sweaty fingers.

"Could fuck you like this forever." Holden angled his face to the side and kissed Bryce's wrist, hips still moving at a torturously slow pace. Bryce's cock had never softened, and it thickened the longer Holden fucked him.

"Can you really come again?"

Holden nodded, eyes hooded.

He did come again, nearly twenty minutes later, both of them sticky and wet and sweaty. Holden reached around and stroked Bryce through another orgasm before he allowed his own, and that one was the end of it. They both collapsed in the mess they'd made of Holden's bed, chests heaving and eyes closed. Holden's dick slipped out of Bryce's ass and a waterfall of cum followed. He was so full of cum, he didn't even need to push it out. He would eventually, but Holden had made sure there was more than enough for Bryce to experience the fullness and the dirtiness in the way he wanted.

"Holden."

Holden hummed, reaching up and grabbing Bryce's hand in his own. He pulled it back and kissed Bryce's knuckles before letting it fall.

"Thank you," Bryce whispered.

Holden made an affirmative noise and let out a long, steady exhale.

"Just give me five more minutes," Holden murmured, "and I'll get you cleaned up."

"Don't want to be clean."

"I know." He pressed his fingertips against Bryce's hole and fucked some of the drying cum back into him. "You'd stay like this forever if you didn't have bills. Naked and full of cum...ready to be filled with more cum."

Bryce's dick twitched at the thought, which was preposterous that his body even thought he'd be able to go again. He could probably do three orgasms under normal circumstances, but what Holden had given him wasn't normal. This was some epic fantasy fulfillment, and he was going to be riding this high for weeks.

"We're a mess, though," Holden went on, kissing Bryce's shoulder. He untangled their bodies and crawled off the bed, standing there naked and gorgeous.

Bryce shifted his weight, rolling toward the other side of the bed to stop Holden before he went too far. He appreciated they had absolutely wrecked the bed, but he was desperate to be close to Holden as he came down from the adrenaline of their fucking.

"Not yet," he pleaded, scraping his fingers across Holden's thigh.

Bryce moved onto all fours, cum sloshing in his belly. It hurt but it felt so fucking good, and he rested his forehead against Holden's stomach to catch his breath.

"Let me suck you," he begged, dragging his nose through Holden's dark happy trail but stopping short of taking Holden's half-soft cock into his mouth. "Let me suck you while I push out this cum. Please."

Holden tangled his fingers into Bryce's hair and angled his face up so Bryce could see him nod. Bryce took Holden's entire length into his mouth, moaning when the soft tip of Holden's cock pressed against the back of his throat. Holden's fingers in his hair were still, guiding not leading, as Bryce hollowed his cheeks and sucked. Holden didn't get much harder, but the sounds he made were enough to keep Bryce going.

"Keep up your end of the deal," Holden coaxed, stretching himself over the arch of Bryce's back to lightly slap his ass. "Make sure you get all of that cum out so I can put more into you later."

Bryce grunted, bearing down and pushing out a trickle of cum that dripped down his balls and onto the bed. Holden thrust gently into his mouth, throwing his head back and moaning softly while Bryce sucked him. There was no urgency between them, no rush. Bryce sucked Holden's cock until his jaw ached and he was certain he'd have to buy Holden a new bed for how much cum he'd pushed out onto the sheets.

When the pressure inside of him eased, Bryce let Holden's cock fall out of his mouth. He collapsed against Holden's stomach, limp and boneless when Holden sat down on the edge of the bed and took Bryce into his arms. Holden kissed the top of his head, whispering things that sounded nice to Bryce's ears, even if they didn't quite make sense to him in that moment. Bryce was able to pick out the confessions of love, the praise over how deep Bryce took Holden's cum, the promises of more...

"Are you with me again?" Holden's mouth was warm against the top of his head, a kiss into his sweaty hair.

"I'm with you forever, I think."

Holden's breath hitched and he tightened his arms around Bryce.

"I don't hate that," Holden said. "But forever needs to start with a warm shower and some fresh sheets."

"A fresh mattress."

Holden stood again, this time helping Bryce to his feet. More cum leaked out of him, and he reached back to cup himself so he didn't ruin Holden's floor on the way to the bathroom.

"This is decidedly unsexy," he muttered, hobbling across the studio apartment and straight into the shower.

Holden chuckled, reaching in and turning the water on for him.

"I think you look good enough to eat," Holden countered. "Flushed and sticky with cum, absolutely wrecked and used. I don't think you've ever looked better."

Bryce rested his head against the back wall of the shower while the water warmed, and he searched Holden's face for any indication the other man was lying. He didn't think Holden would do that, but Bryce also understood what Holden had done for him was a little bit out of the norm and far beyond something basic like handcuffs and spanking.

"Are you good in here on your own?" Holden asked. "I'm going to strip the bed."

"I'll be good," he said.

Holden watched him a second longer before stepping away from the shower and shutting the bathroom door behind him. Bryce closed his eyes, covering his face with his hands while the hot water rained down on him. He couldn't believe that had just happened. Groaning, he reached behind him and felt the tender circumference of his hole, pushing more cum out onto his fingertips. Eventually he would get rid of the fake stuff and get to Holden's actual seed, but he also hoped Holden had spent far enough inside of him that the real stuff might stay up there until the morning. He stopped trying to empty himself, then washed up and turned off the shower.

He made one last attempt to empty himself before wrapping a towel around his waist and shuffling out of the bathroom. The bed, when he went to get clean underwear, looked pristine, like they'd never even laid on it, let alone fucked on it. The new sheets were hunter green, and Holden had even changed the pillowcases. Bryce danced his fingers across the soft cotton before heading for the kitchen where he heard Holden working.

He caught up to his boyfriend at the counter, one plate in front of him stacked high with cubed cheese and crackers and sliced lunch meat. Bryce hadn't been hungry, but at the sight of the snack tray, his stomach growled. More cum leaked out of him and he groaned, dropping his head back.

"I already put a towel on the couch," Holden said, grabbing the plate and a glass of water. "You're fine."

They sat together on the couch, the food on Holden's lap and the water in Bryce's hand. Bryce nestled himself against Holden's side, eating slowly and enjoying the soft caress of Holden's fingers against the outside of his arm. Bryce stared at their reflection in the dark TV screen, wondering how he'd gotten so lucky.

"Are you okay?" Holden asked, breath ruffling Bryce's hair.

"Better than. That was…that was everything."

"As good as you imagined?"

"Better." He angled his face up for a kiss, which Holden gave him without being asked. "How are you?"

"I'm perfect."

They ate a while longer, quiet in the companionable and safe silence of Holden's apartment. Bryce's lashes fluttered and he passed the water to Holden without another word. Holden set the water and the plate on the coffee table, and then opened his arms to Bryce, who burrowed against his chest like he wanted to get under Holden's skin. He did, in a way. Not a creepy way, but in a connected way. Holden seemed to sense the need, still lingering from before. He held Bryce steady and sure until Bryce fell into a calm and peaceful sleep.

CHAPTER 21
Holden

HOLDEN WAS NOT LOOKING FORWARD to work on Tuesday, and Merrick was already at the shop by the time Holden arrived. He took a deep breath to center himself, unlocked the front door, and stepped inside. The bells on the door handle jingled, and Holden checked the clock to decide if he should lock the door from the inside or leave it ready for the day. It was five minutes before eleven, so he shoved his keys into his pocket and went straight to his station. He sat down and rolled his stool into the strip of space that separated his and Merrick's station.

"Let's hear it," he said, scratching at a persistent itch on the side of his nose that wouldn't go away.

"What?"

Holden made a broad gesture with his hand. "About seeing your brother behind your back."

Merrick blinked at him slowly, apparently at a loss for words…for what absolutely had to be the first time ever in Holden's experience.

"I said what I had to say when I texted you," Merrick answered.

"What?"

Merrick rolled himself over to the middle space, his knees brushing past Holden's as he slid in front of him.

"Would any of it make a difference?" Merrick asked. "If I said I didn't want you to be with him?"

Holden's body reacted viscerally, a sharp twitch of his shoulders at the thought of never having Bryce in his arms again.

"No."

"Then what's the point?"

Holden wasn't sure what to say. It was more common for him to be speechless, but Merrick still laughed at him just the same.

"You like him?"

"Yes."

I love him, Holden thought.

"Do you treat him well?"

"Yes."

"Does he treat you well?"

"Of course," Holden answered. "Why wouldn't he?"

Merrick grimaced, bouncing his head from side to side like he had something to say but was again, for the second time in his life, not willing to say it. Holden provided the answer for them both. "I know you think your brother is...I don't know, a slut or something."

He hated to use that word, but it was the most accurate one to what Merrick had, on more than one occasion, implied.

"He's not," Holden said. "I mean, maybe he was before, but not with me."

"I like working here is all," Merrick said. "I don't want him to mess up my work."

Holden bristled, failing to make the correlation. "How would that happen?"

"If he does something bad to you," Merrick explained.

"What if I do something bad to him?" Holden suggested. "What if I'm the one who ruins it?"

Just the thought of losing Bryce was a knife in his chest, but he had to play through the hypothetical situation to prove his point to Merrick.

"Why would you?"

"Why would he?"

Merrick sighed heavily, shrugging. "I just want him to be happy, and I also want to be happy. I'm happy working here."

"And he's happy being with me," Holden said. "But you should talk to him about that."

"Don't need to," Merrick said with a laugh.

"Oh, so you save all your talking for me?"

"This is the most I've ever heard you say, now that you mention it, but no. I sent him a text a lot like the one I sent you, and we're already good. Bryce knows me, knows how I am."

"He knows you love him," Holden supplied.

Merrick nodded, and the upstairs door to Riggs's apartment opened. "So we're good?"

Holden held out his hand and Merrick shook it. "We're good."

"Who's good?" Riggs asked, coming downstairs and tugging a hoodie over his head.

"Holden is sleeping with my brother," Merrick announced, wheeling his stool back to the other side of his station.

Holden's cheeks burned, and he rolled back to his side while doing his best to avoid Riggs's curious stare.

"That's…something," Riggs said.

Holden nodded, pulling his phone out of his pocket to text Bryce. He had no idea when the conversation between Bryce and Merrick had taken place, but it couldn't have been too long ago. Bryce had spent the whole weekend at Holden's apartment, mostly in various stages of undress with varying volumes of cum inside of his body, and it was with the most reluctance that Holden had peeled himself away from his boyfriend to come to work and face his brother.

> things are good here with Merrick

Bryce sent him back a selfie, lounging on Holden's couch with one arm folded behind his head. He wasn't wearing a shirt and he hadn't shaved the whole time they'd been together. Three days of scruff lined Bryce's jaw, and it was less than two hours ago Holden had nibbled his way from Bryce's chin to his ear, their bodies pressed together still naked and warm.

> BRYCE
>
> knew they would be.
>
> I love your couch btw.

Holden typed out a message and hesitated before sending it, only to delete it and rewrite it three times before he finally found the courage to press the send button. Off it went and Holden set his phone face down on his station before Bryce had any time to reply.

"Merrick, what're your books like today?" Riggs asked, frowning down at his own phone. The look didn't necessarily mean something was wrong; Riggs just generally had that look about him unless his boyfriend Smith was around.

"Slow afternoon, but I've got a few later in the day. Was planning to catch up on some sketches for next week, but I was also thinking of trying to get better at watercolors. I don't really know." Merrick rattled on and Holden rolled his eyes, staring at his cell phone like it was a bomb about to detonate.

"Smith said he was going to bring his best friend by the shop for a tattoo."

"Let's do it." Merrick grinned and clapped his hands together. "What would he want?"

"No idea." Riggs sent a message on his phone and returned it to his pocket. "Smith is with her, but I told them to come by whenever they were ready."

"Perfect. I guess I don't really have enough time to get into watercolors today then, but sketching will probably work."

Holden's phone vibrated with an incoming message and he sucked in a breath, his hand hovering over the device before he picked it up again. He shouldn't have sent the message. It had been rushed and poorly thought out, and Bryce was going to hate the idea and probably break up with him for it.

That seemed dramatic as he played the scenario out in his head, but it was still possible. Maybe just not in this timeline. Bryce, for whatever reason, loved him, and he loved Bryce in return. Holden would have never picked a man like Bryce for himself, but maybe that was why he'd been single for so long. He'd been looking for the wrong people, or maybe he'd simply been waiting for Bryce.

His phone started to vibrate again, this time with an incoming call, not a text. He flipped the phone over to see Bryce's name on the screen and he answered the call with his eyes closed. Holden stood and headed for the front of the shop, ducking under the counter before stepping through the door and onto the sidewalk.

"Hello."

Holden leaned against the outside wall of the building, one leg bent and the other straight, his foot pressed against the plain wall of the shop. The stucco could use some color. It was a shame Riggs had left it unpainted for so long. Holden would have to talk to Riggs about a mural or something. It could be a fun side project for him and Merrick to do.

"You didn't answer my text," Bryce said.

"I've been scared to look at it," he admitted.

"Why?"

"Old habits, I imagine."

Bryce chuckled softly in his ear. "Do you want to read it while I'm on the phone or do you want me to tell you what I said?"

Holden closed his eyes and dropped his head against the wall. "You might as well tell me."

It was a warm day, the sun already beating down on the top of his head, his legs warm beneath the black denim of his jeans. The nerves and the cold sweat didn't help things either.

"I think your apartment might be too small for two people," Bryce said, and Holden's heart sank.

"You're right, it was a stu—"

"Holden, stop talking."

He did, clicking his teeth together as he snapped his mouth closed. He could still picture Bryce on his couch, naked or nearly naked, sweat glistening on the center of his chest and the gorgeous pink flush he got when he exerted himself.

"It might be too small for two people," Bryce repeated, "but maybe not for us."

"What?"

"I don't have a lot of things of my own."

"Bryce."

"I don't think I'd take up too much room."

"You can take all of it," Holden said quickly, heart back in place and ready to run a damn marathon.

"I don't want it all," Bryce said. "Only enough."

"It's yours."

Bryce paused. "Holden, we've only known each other a few weeks, are you sure you want me to move in with you?"

He was as certain of it now as he had been when he sent the text, as he had been when he fell asleep the night before staring at a cluster of freckles on Bryce's cheek that he'd never seen before.

"Very sure," he said. "Besides, you already have a key and spend more time there than me."

"Do you want to tell Merrick or me?"

Holden laughed at that, angling his head toward the front of the shop in time to see Smith walking up, accompanied by a gorgeous woman with shiny brown hair and flawless skin. She must be the best friend Riggs had mentioned.

"He's about to tattoo Riggs's boyfriend's best friend," Holden said, pushing off the wall and heading back to the door. "I'll tell him."

"That's mean."

"What time will you be home from work tonight?"

"Late, but you don't have to wait up."

"You don't have to tell me what to do." Holden stepped back into the shop and slipped under the counter. "I'll talk to you soon."

"Can't wait."

Holden disconnected the call and tapped his fingers on Merrick's chair as he walked by. "Your brother is moving in with me."

Merrick's head snapped up, his face a mask of confusion. Holden smiled, and the door opened again. He didn't need to look to know it was Smith and the distraction he'd been hoping for when he told Merrick the news. The two of them studied each other while Riggs made his greetings to Smith.

"Is he now?" Merrick asked. "His idea?"

"Mine."

Merrick made a pleased sound. "Who am I to argue with anything my brother does, right?"

"Right."

"Merrick," Riggs called out. "Come meet Asha."

Holden observed the introductions, waiting until Merrick was deep in conversation with Asha about what sort of tattoo she wanted to get and what the time would look like to get it done to send another text to Bryce.

I think he took it well.

BRYCE

I thought I took it well.

Holden's tongue stuck to the roof of his mouth.

No one takes it better than you.

Go get your things this afternoon. I want you moved in before I get home from work.

Who's needy now??

Please do what you're told?

Are you asking or telling?

Do what you're told.

I don't think I should like this as much as I do, but I shouldn't like a lot of things as much as I do.

Is that a yes?

Yes, I'll fully invade your space before I leave for work tonight.

Do you like that?

I love it.

I love you.

CHAPTER 22

Bryce

THINGS WITH MERRICK went the way they always had. Half of an apology and a promise to listen better in the future. Bryce knew it wasn't ideal, but that had always been the resolution to disagreements with his brother. He reminded himself of that as he packed the few things he'd scattered across Merrick's guest room and put them in the back seat of his car. He'd really left home with the clothes on his back and not much else. It was still well before dinner by the time he got everything unpacked into Holden's studio, but he was hungry just the same. Bryce made himself a sandwich and ate it standing at the counter, trying to make sense of the whirlwind his life had become since the plane touched down in LA.

Even though Bryce enjoyed bartending at Rapture, especially when he worked alongside Callum, his shift passed at a snail's pace. He was just too eager to get back to Holden's place…to his place.

Their place.

It was right before three when he slid the key into the lock and let himself in. The lights in the apartment were off, but

Holden was on the couch, fully dressed down to the sneakers, his face illuminated by his phone.

"Everything okay?" Bryce asked, lingering in the doorway.

Holden jumped up from the couch and shoved his phone into his pocket, joining Bryce at the door.

"You're just in time. Let's go."

Before he could argue, Holden grabbed him and yanked him back out of the apartment and down the hall. They reached the stairwell and instead of going down, Holden led him up and up and up until they were on the roof of the building. The wind was cooler that high, and Holden wrapped his arm around Bryce's shoulder without being asked. Bryce had no idea what was happening, but he still let Holden usher him to the ledge where two patio chairs were open and waiting for them.

"What are we doing?" Bryce asked, taking a seat for himself, just like Holden.

"Stardust," Holden said, reaching over and taking Bryce's hand in his, the one with the D-U-S-T across his knuckles. Holden kissed each letter, then angled his face toward the sky. "There's some planetary alignment. Jupiter and Saturn and Mars, I think. I saw it and paid more attention to the time, not the names."

Bryce chuckled, vision going a little soft around the edges. They didn't have a telescope so they probably wouldn't be able to see anything, but no thought had ever counted more.

"I love you so much," he blurted, and Holden answered him with a shy smile. Holden tucked his chin toward his chest and a few strands of hair fell into his eyes, making him look young and bashful, and Bryce was out of his chair before he could think better of it.

He straddled Holden, grabbed his face and kissed him hard. The move seemed to startle Holden, but he recovered quickly and returned the kiss, melting against the back of the chair when Bryce pressed their bodies together.

"The sun is going to come up soon," Holden murmured against his lips. "As much as I want more of this, can you see anything? Can you show me?"

Bryce reluctantly unfolded himself from Holden's lap, but before he could move back to his own chair, Holden yanked him down onto his lap and looped his arms around Bryce's stomach. Holden rested his chin on Bryce's shoulder and the two of them turned their attention toward the sky.

"The red one is Mercury," Bryce said, not even needing to point. "The big bright one is probably Jupiter, so I would assume the other one in line with them is Saturn."

Holden made a contented sound in his ear.

"It's wild we can see them from here."

"Wild we're made of the same stuff as they are," Bryce countered.

Holden brushed his lips across Bryce's ear, and Bryce shivered, pressing himself harder against Holden's chest.

"At work today, I was listening to Asha talk to Smith about Riggs," Holden said.

"Asha?"

"Smith's best friend. The one Merrick tattooed."

"Right. Okay."

Holden tightened his arms around Bryce's waist. "She was giving him a hard time about how he fell off the face of the planet when he met Riggs. How the only thing that mattered to Smith in those early days was being with his man."

Bryce smiled and searched out the stars of Orion's belt, looking for a constellation he knew by heart while Holden spoke softly into his ear.

"They're still like that. Obsessed with each other and attached."

"Like us?"

Holden made an agreeable noise. "It made me feel like this was okay. With you."

"Was it not before?"

"It was, but…"

"It felt okay for us," Bryce guessed, "not for everyone else's perception of us."

"Something like that." Holden closed his mouth and left a featherlight kiss against Bryce's neck.

"Do you believe in fate?"

Holden nodded, chin digging into Bryce's shoulder.

"Is that what this is?"

Another nod.

Bryce inhaled and let a comfortable silence fall. Down on the street, there was hardly any traffic to be heard, no one out walking yet. The sun was still hours away from cresting the eastern horizon and Holden's arms gave him more peace than Bryce had ever known.

"Are you cold?" Holden asked him later, words rough for how long they'd sat in silence with each other.

"A little."

"Let's go inside. I'll warm you up."

Bryce crawled off Holden's lap, fighting the shiver that slammed into him from being fully exposed to the early morning air. "Was that an innuendo?"

"Not this time." Holden took his hand and left their chairs, a stoic invitation for return.

They walked together back into the apartment and locked the door behind them. Holden and Bryce stripped each other naked in the entryway, leaving a trail of clothes and socks in their wake. Roaming hands turned to rough grabs and soft kisses, and then Holden took him right to bed, pressed him down into the sheets and kissed him hard against the back of his neck.

"It would be hot, by the way," Bryce murmured, the words trailing off into a yawn.

"What would be hot?" Holden smiled against his neck, teeth cool against Bryce's flushed skin.

"I think sometimes about waking up with you inside of me," he admitted, another sexual interest he'd never shared with anyone. "Like you were so overcome you couldn't even wait to wake me up."

Holden let his hand trail down Bryce's bare hip and over the swell of his ass. He stopped short of touching Bryce's hole.

"I'll keep that in mind," Holden promised. "We have years ahead of us, don't we?"

"I hope so."

Bryce's lashes fluttered closed, and Holden nestled his half-hard cock between Bryce's ass cheeks.

"We have plenty of time to explore every possible way to get you off," he said, "And after that, I think we can probably still find some more."

"I've got to be honest. I like it when you talk, Holden."

"I like it when you talk too."

Bryce angled his head back and chased after a kiss, which Holden freely gave, and then Bryce fell asleep, content and loved, cocooned in the arms of the man who loved him as he was, and as he'd ever be.

Ink and Ember continues in August of 2026 with Merrick.

Or backtrack to the beginning to meet Riggs and Smith in Breaking the Mold.

Join my newsletter to learn more about Club Rapture and stay up to date on new releases, sales, and more.

Also by Kate Hawthorne

Ink and Ember

Holden

Merrick

Toren

Club Rapture: Risk Aware

Love by Design

Burden of Proof

Breaking the Mold

By All Accounts

Club Rapture: Giving Consent

Worth the Risk

Worth the Wait

Worth the Fight

Worth the Chance

Trophy Doms Social Club

Humbled

Edged

Praised

Bound

Shared

Trophy Doms New York

All In

Secrets in Edgewood: The Complete Series

The Lonely Hearts Stories

His Kind of Love

The Colors Between Us

Love Comes After

Until You Say Otherwise

<u>STANDALONES</u>

Rebound

One for the Road

Daybreak - Vino & Veritas

Unfettered

Dreams

A Thousand Lifetimes

<u>COLLABORATIONS</u>

With E.M. Denning

Irreplaceable

Future Fake Husband

Future Gay Boyfriend

Future Ex Enemy

About Kate Hawthorne

Kate Hawthorne is an author of character-driven LGBT romance, known for crafting emotionally intense stories with high heat and a kinky twist. Creating worlds where passion and angst collide, Kate's books bring you complex protagonists in fearless pursuit of self-exploration and happy —if not sometimes unconventional—endings for everyone.

Visit her website
http://www.katehawthornebooks.com

Sign up for Kate's newsletter
http://www.katehawthornebooks.com/extra

patreon.com/katehawthorne
instagram.com/kate.hawthorne
threads.com/@kate.hawthorne
facebook.com/authorkatehawthorne